Toots

Underground

Also by Carol Hughes

Toots and the Upside-Down House
Jack Black & the Ship of Thieves

CAROL HUGHES

RANDOM HOUSE 🏠 NEW YORK

Text copyright © 1998 by Carol Hughes.

Cover art copyright © 2001 by Greg Newbold.

All rights reserved under International and Pan-American Copyright Conventions.

Published in the United States by Random House, Inc., New York.

Originally published in Great Britain by Bloomsbury Publishing Plc in 1998.

First American edition, 2001.

www.randomhouse.com/kids

Library of Congress Cataloging-in-Publication Data
Hughes, Carol.
Toots underground / by Carol Hughes.
    p. cm.
SUMMARY: Toots is once again transported to the Upside-Down World, where the
fairy inhabitants are desperately trying to defeat the evil waspgnat before it destroys
the garden that Toots and the fairies share.
ISBN 0-375-81086-2 (trade) — ISBN 0-375-91086-7 (lib. bdg.)
[1. Fairies—Fiction. 2. Gardens—Fiction.] I. Title. PZ7.H873116 Tq 2001
[Fic]—dc21   00-51766

Printed in the United States of America   September 2001   10 9 8 7 6 5 4 3 2 1

RANDOM HOUSE and colophon are registered trademarks of Random House, Inc.

For Mum and Ron

CONTENTS

A Short Note
on the Upside Down-ness of It All

Every house has an Upside-Down House and every garden an Upside-Down Garden, in much the same way that every school has an Upside-Down School and every playground an Upside-Down Playground.

"What is all this upside down-ness?" you may ask. It's just what it sounds like. The same place, but upside down. Only it isn't really the same place at all. You'd never know it was there unless you stood on your head, or hung backward over a chair, because that's the only way you can see it.

When you first look at the world upside down, it will probably look like nothing special at all, and you'll wonder what on earth I'm talking about. But if you're patient and quiet, you might see something you didn't expect to see sauntering across the ceiling or sitting on the bottom of a tree branch. And that's when you'll know you've seen someone or something from the Upside-Down World. Go on, try it now. Turn yourself the other way up and stare down at the ceiling or the sky and imagine what it would be like if the world was always that way up. What would happen if you fell into those clouds? You would probably fall forever.

But—and here's the catch—if you've ever been to the Upside-Down World, you won't remember, because although at the time everything seems very real, when you return to your own world, the memory fades like a dream. That was how it was for Toots. She could barely remember Olive and the fairies and everything that had happened to her in the Upside-Down House. That was until she met Olive again.

Toots

Underground

1 SPRING

One bright, blustery April afternoon, Toots sat on the swing in her garden and shivered. Even though the sun was shining, a wintry wind rattled through the fence. It screamed across the lawn and shook the bare branches of the horse chestnut tree and sometimes it sounded as though it was laughing—a nasty, high-pitched laugh. Toots zipped up her jacket and shivered again.

She grabbed hold of the swing's ropes, pressed her bottom back against the seat, and kicked off. By stretching her legs out in front of her, then folding them back in, she swung higher and higher toward the sky.

From the swing Toots could see Jemma's house. Jemma had been Toots's best friend ever since she'd moved into the house across the street, but since Christmas Jemma had been acting strangely and Toots didn't like it. Jemma would promise to come over to play and then wouldn't, or she'd plan to go to the beach with Toots and then at the last minute say she couldn't go.

Then there was yesterday, the day of the car wash. Toots pushed the swing higher. Washing cars to make extra pocket money had been all Jemma's idea in the first place, and together they'd arranged to wash six neighbors' cars. But yesterday morning Jemma had mysteriously disappeared, and Toots had had to wash all the cars by herself. It had taken her till teatime.

Then this morning when Jemma had come round, she hadn't offered an explanation. She hadn't said she was sorry. She just acted as though nothing had happened. And when Toots asked her where she'd been, Jemma had just shrugged and shifted from foot to foot, then tried to change the subject.

"Do you want to come to my house and play?" Jemma had asked. But Toots had shaken her head.

"No. My dad wants me to stay in," Toots had lied. "Bye." Toots had shut the front door and watched through the peephole as Jemma crossed the road to her house.

Toots leaned back on the swing. She turned her face to the sky and tried not to think about Jemma. Instead, she focused on the horse chestnut tree. There was something so sad about it. It should have been in bud, but there wasn't a new leaf in sight. The bare branches reached out forlornly to the

April sky as though they were searching for spring.

It wasn't just the tree, Toots realized. The whole garden was still bare, even though she and her father had planted hundreds of bulbs. In all the other gardens on their street, spring flowers were already nodding beneath the trees, but in Toots's garden there wasn't a crocus, nor a daffodil, nor a tulip, nor a hyacinth to be seen.

Toots's father had been so worried that he'd asked Mr. Phelps, the tree surgeon, to come and take a look. Toots had stood beside her father while Mr. Phelps, a tall man with a long red nose and bright eyes, had examined the roots, trunk, branches, and twigs of the horse chestnut tree.

He'd jabbed a stick into the soil at the foot of the tree and stared down into the hole he'd made. His sharp blue eyes seemed to burn into the earth as though he could see right through the hard brown dirt to the layers below.

"This tree's dying, all right," he'd said, patting the trunk with the flat of his hand. He crouched down and picked up a pinch of soil. He rubbed it in his fingers and sniffed it, then dropped it and stood up. "It looks like the roots are poisoning the whole garden. That's why nothing's coming up anywhere."

"Can you do anything to save it?" Toots's dad asked.

"The tree?" Mr. Phelps shook his head. "The

garden, maybe, but the tree'll have to come down, and the sooner the better. It'll be a shame to lose such a beauty."

"Yes, it will," Toots's father had said. He sighed as he stared up into the lattice of dark twigs. Toots looked up too and saw a raven's nest swaying in the uppermost branches. She slipped her hand inside her father's and gave his fingers a squeeze. He squeezed hers back and smiled down at her. It was one of his "don't worry" smiles, but she knew he was upset.

Toots tried to imagine what the garden would look like when the magnificent tree was gone. It would leave such a terrible space. She remembered how the tree had looked every spring with its new green leaves as big as dishcloths hanging out to dry. She remembered the blossoms fat as church candles swaying in the summer breeze and the huge conkers that fell all over the lawn in autumn. She always had the best conkers at school and plenty to share, but next fall she wouldn't have any.

She kicked out with her feet. She could almost touch the branches with her toes. It was one of her favorite games. She could never quite reach. Maybe next year when she'd grown—but next year there wouldn't be a tree. Mr. Phelps was going to come and chop it down tomorrow afternoon. Toots stopped trying to reach the branches and let the swing slow down.

If only, she thought, looking at the bleak, wintry garden. *If only there was some way to save the tree.*

A scratching at the back door made Toots look round. Binky wanted to come out. Binky was Mrs. Willets's dog, and he accompanied her every day when she came to look after Toots. Toots's mother had died a long time ago, and Toots was used to other people looking after her during school holidays.

Binky looked about a hundred years old, mostly because one of his eyes was cloudy and white. He was small with red fur, stumpy legs, and pointed ears that were too big for his head. Binky loved digging. His holes were all over the flower beds and the lawn. They were everywhere, in fact, except in the crazy-paving patio Toots's father had put in last month.

As for Mrs. Willets, she was as wrinkled as a raisin, and her black hair was streaked with gray. She wasn't much of one for playing or going out anywhere. She liked to watch television. Toots's father left for work every day at eight in the morning. As soon as he was gone, *ping!* On went the television, and on it stayed till he came home. Mrs. Willets usually brought sandwiches for Toots and herself so that she didn't have to get up in the middle of one of her programs to make lunch. Toots took her sandwiches outside and shared them with Binky, which made Binky think that Toots was his long-lost sister.

As soon as Toots opened the back door, Binky shot out into the garden, barking happily.

"No digging, Binky," warned Toots as she climbed back on the swing. It was as much use as telling a bee not to buzz. Binky went straight to the flower beds and began to dig. Toots jumped off the swing.

"No!" she cried, grabbing hold of his collar. "Naughty! You know that's not allowed!" But Binky already had his nose down a hole and was fighting hard to keep it there. With an enormous effort Toots pulled him away and, fixing his lead to his collar, tied the other end to the leg of the swing.

"Stay!" she commanded. Obedient at last, Binky lay on the ground with his nose stretched as close as possible to the nearest hole. He sniffed and whimpered while Toots returned to the swing.

"Sorry, Bink, but you were warned," she said.

Suddenly, Binky barked and rolled over. He lay very still with his paws dangling over his chest and one ear flopped inside out. Only his eyes moved, flitting back and forth. Toots cocked her head and looked sideways at the broad tree trunk to see what he was looking at. Nothing seemed out of the ordinary. She leaned farther over but still couldn't see anything.

Binky barked again and wagged his tail. Determined to get to the bottom of the mystery, Toots clung to the swing's ropes and leaned all the way over until her head was down between her legs and she was looking at the garden and the rest of the world upside down.

That was when she saw the tiny blue creature no bigger than a ladybug standing on the underside of the swing. Toots narrowed her eyes. There was something very familiar about this tiny creature, but what? Then the creature lifted what looked like a miniature megaphone to her lips, and Toots suddenly remembered everything. All her memories of the Upside-Down World came flooding back.

"Olive!" she cried before the tiny creature had had a chance to say a word. "Olive, is that you?"

2 DOWNSIDE UP AGAIN

"Thank heavens, Toots!" boomed Cadet Fairy Olive Brown through the megaphone. "I've been calling for you all morning! I thought you'd never hear me. If it wasn't for your doggy friend over there, I don't think you'd ever have thought to look beneath the swing."

Toots smiled. The last time she'd seen her tiny friend, Olive had just earned her wings and been promoted to the Upside-Down Garden. Before that, Olive had been an ordinary cadet house fairy, no wings or anything. Toots grinned. Olive had looked so lovely that day in the attic, her face beaming with pride as all the other fairies clapped and hooted. It was funny how sharp the memory seemed now.

"Olive?" said Toots softly, mindful of how sensitive tiny ears are to the sounds of the big world. "I don't know why, but until just now I think I'd forgotten you, I'd forgotten the Upside-Down World, I'd forgotten *everything*."

"That's what happens," called Olive through the megaphone. "You can't help it. Once you're right way up, you soon forget all about us, but not to worry. The important thing is that you've seen me. I've got so much to tell you. Something terrible is happening. Look!"

Olive gestured toward the garden, and for the first time Toots noticed what it looked like upside down. It was a shock. The air was full of strange white dust. It was as though it was snowing, but upside down! The dust covered the underside of everything in the garden. It collected beneath rocks and pebbles and lay as thick as snow on the underside of the branches of the horse chestnut tree. The garden looked as though it was still buried deep in winter. The white powder even covered the underside of the swing. It had settled on Olive's head and shoulders and lay so deep that it covered her feet.

Toots lifted her head. From right way up she couldn't see any of the snowy dust at all. She turned upside down again.

"We need your help," said Olive. "If you're not busy, could you come and see what you can do?"

"Of course," Toots replied. "But I'll have to be back before my father gets home."

"I'll make sure you are," replied Olive.

"All right. What shall I do?"

Olive paused for a moment. "Let me think. I've never done this outside before. It could be tricky. . . . Oh, I know. You kneel on the swing and grip the seat, that'll be the best way."

Toots took a deep breath and grabbed the wooden seat with both hands, then bent over till she could see Olive.

"Oh, wait a minute," said Olive. "I almost forgot the most important bit." Fluttering her wings, Olive flew off the edge of the swing and tied a length of fine cobweb about Toots's wrist. Olive waved cheerily and lifted the megaphone to her lips once more.

"The cobweb will act as a safety rope just in case you . . . well, you know. It could be tricky when your gravity switches over—that is, when everything that was up becomes down, and vice versa. I'm not sure when that will happen, so you'd better not let go of the swing at all. If you're not holding on properly, your weight could pull us both into the sky, and that would be disastrous."

Toots looked at the sky and shuddered. She remembered how it had been when Olive had first taken her to the Upside-Down World. But that had been inside, in the living room. When Toots's gravity had switched there, she'd fallen to the ceiling. Now there was no ceiling to catch her. If she fell here, she would fall forever.

"Ready?" asked Olive, who was letting out a good length of the cobweb rope.

Toots gulped, then nodded. "Ready," she replied, though in truth she wasn't sure if she was or not.

Olive took a deep breath and yanked on the rope. Toots felt it tug at her wrist. At first nothing happened. Then, almost imperceptibly, Toots felt the wooden seat growing thicker in her hands. Soon it was so thick she had to let go with her thumbs and could only hold on with her fingers. The wood became rough and full of large splinters. Toots shifted her knees, and the swing shuddered.

"Steady there!" Olive called from beneath the swing. Toots winced.

"Sorry," she said.

Toots peered over the edge of the seat. Olive grinned at her and nodded encouragingly. The megaphone hung on a strap around her neck. Olive lifted it to her lips with her free hand.

"Soon have you here, safe and sound," she said.

Toots nodded and concentrated on holding on as best she could. As she got smaller, Toots could see Olive more and more clearly. It was lovely to see Olive's big, red, friendly face again. Olive was wearing a new uniform—a shimmering metallic-blue flying suit and a matching helmet with thick straps that fastened under her chin. Toots guessed that the uniform's shimmery blue color was some sort of camouflage. The whole effect was very smart and made Olive look like a large bluebottle fly. A silver bucket dangled from a hook on Olive's belt. Toots noticed that it was different from the one Olive had had as a house fairy. This one had a lid that fastened with a little catch. Toots wondered why. But she forgot all about the bucket when she noticed Olive's pretty gossamer wings fluttering behind her back.

"Olive!" exclaimed Toots. "Your wings! They look fantastic."

"Do you think so?" squeaked Olive, not bothering with the megaphone now that Toots was small enough to hear her properly. She beamed with pride and fluttered her wings so that they sparkled in the sun.

A distant shout made them both look over to the tree. Toots could now see dozens of fairies in bluebottle uniforms flying frantically through the blizzard. They were snatching at the feathery flakes and putting them into their buckets.

"Toots, concentrate!" said Olive, giving the cobweb rope a tug and bracing herself on the swing. "Your gravity could switch at any time."

And suddenly, with an incredible jolt, it did.

All at once the world turned upside down. Toots screamed as her legs fell out from under her, and she found herself hanging by her fingertips with her feet dangling down toward the sky.

"Hold on, Toots!" gasped Olive. "You're still too

heavy! I can't take all your weight. Don't let go of the swing, or you'll pull us both down!"

Toots tried not to panic. As her hands shrank, she found it harder and harder to hold on to the swing. Even worse, Toots's shift in gravity had started the swing rocking violently. She did everything she could to keep her hold, but everything was not enough. Toots screamed as her hands slipped and she plummeted toward the sky.

"Toots!" cried Olive. The fairy dug her heels into the swing and flapped her wings furiously, but Toots was still too heavy for her, and she was dragged right across the wooden seat.

Luckily, just before Olive reached the edge of the swing, the cobweb rope caught fast in one of the large splinters at the edge of the seat. Toots jerked to a stop and cried out in pain. It felt as though her arm was going to be pulled out of its socket.

Olive quickly secured her end of the rope around a nail head. "Toots!" she shouted as she leapt off the swing. "Hold on! I'm coming!"

Olive looped her arm around Toots's waist. "Try and climb up the rope," she puffed. "I can't take all your weight, but I'll do what I can."

With Olive's help, Toots climbed the rope hand over hand, trying not to think of the miles of air beneath her. A few moments later she pulled herself onto the underside of the swing and lay up to her ears in the thick white powder, trying to recover her breath.

"That was close," puffed Olive as she untied the cobweb rope from Toots's wrist and wound it in a neat coil. Toots sat up and stared across the garden at the house, which loomed upside down in the distance. She picked up a handful of the white powder and found that it wasn't a powder at all, but thousands of small, white, feathery seed carriers like those from a dandelion clock.

"What is this stuff?" she asked, tossing a handful into the air and watching as it floated prettily down.

"Oh, no, Toots, don't disturb it," said Olive, frantically waving her arms up and down to try to get the feathers to settle faster. "We're trying to keep it under control." She picked up a tiny feather and held it out to Toots. "These are the furzeweed seed heads. See, most are harmless, because we've already removed the seeds." Olive picked up another feather. "But look, here's one that almost got away." She plucked a tiny seed off the feathery stalk, put the seed in her bucket, and shut the lid. "It's nearly an impossible task. You can see from the state of the garden that there's very little time."

Toots ran her hands through the feathers and found another with its seed still attached. She yanked the seed free. It was like a tiny pearl in the palm of her hand.

"Is this why the plants won't grow?" Toots asked. "Is this why the horse chestnut tree is dying?"

"Yes, partly," replied Olive in a distant voice. Toots looked up. Olive was staring out at the garden. "But furzeweed wouldn't behave like this by itself. The only way to save the garden is to get to the root of the problem." Olive stared for a moment more, then shook herself. She smiled and winked at Toots. "That's why you're here! Come on, the group captain will be waiting." Olive set her hands on her hips and looked one way, then the other. "Now, where's the best place to take off from?" She licked her finger and held it up into the wind. "Nor' nor'west I think." She pulled a spare pair of goggles out of her bucket and handed them to Toots.

Toots pulled on the goggles and stood up. She looked for somewhere to put the furzeweed seed but, finding nowhere suitable, dropped it into her pocket.

"Good, it looks like you've stopped shrinking at last," said Olive. "I should be able to carry you easily now. I'll fly as steadily as I can."

Toots measured herself against Olive's shoulder. "I must have grown since the last time I saw you," she said. Then she laughed. "Or you're shrinking, Olive. But that's impossible, isn't it?"

"Not at all," said Olive. "I *am* shrinking. Garden fairies are always smaller than house fairies, in the same way that river fairies are smaller than garden fairies and sky fairies are smaller than everyone. And in every unit the highest-ranked fairies are the smallest of all. It stands to reason. I've been shrinking ever since I graduated from the Upside-Down House. By the way, I hope you don't get airsick."

"I don't think I do," said Toots.

Olive tapped her finger against her chin as she stared thoughtfully along the length of the swing. "I don't think a standing start's a good idea," she said as she popped her goggles over her eyes and fastened the strap on her helmet. "It's probably best if you start running, then I'll fly over and pick you up. How does that sound?"

It sounded dangerous, but Toots had promised to try to help. Resolutely she pulled her goggles down over her eyes and began to run. She was halfway across the swing when Olive's arms looped around her middle and lifted her up toward the garden.

Toots gasped. Flying upside down was wonderful! Below them the sky was full of fat clouds, some white, some gold. Above them the garden lay stark and bare and full of winter.

Olive flew swiftly, circling over the crazy paving with its oddly shaped tiles, then past the fishpond with its bright mirror reflecting the sky, and on toward the horse chestnut tree. They soon passed all the other fairies, who were busily filling their buckets with tiny white seeds.

Olive swooped around the tree. Just as they came to the far side, Toots looked up and saw Binky break free from his leash and come bounding across the grass toward them. The fairies scattered.

"Watch out for Binky!" cried Toots.

"Poor Binky," laughed Olive as she veered sharply to the left. "He doesn't mean any harm. He just wants to play. He can smell us, but he can't see us, unless he turns upside down."

Olive changed direction again and flew sharply up toward a dark hole between the tree's roots. On one side of the hole there was a long, dark scar shaped like the number three.

In an instant they were inside the dark tunnel, the day disappearing behind them. Toots looked back and saw the tip of Binky's snout crammed into the hole. *So that's why he's always digging*, she thought. *He knows there's something down here.*

The tunnel was dark, but Toots wasn't afraid. She felt safe, the way you always feel with an old friend.

Far ahead of them there was a light, which grew brighter as they approached. Toots could see now that they were not alone in the tunnel. Other fairies flew past in the darkness, and Toots could hear the flapping of their wings close by.

"Almost at the landing bay!" shouted Olive above the noise of so many wings. No sooner had she said this than they burst into a large, vaulted cave with smooth, curved walls. Stretching out before them were two long runways with blinking colored lights along the edges. At the far end of the room were two large metal doors. The doors stood open, and fairies filed in and out.

It was all go in the landing bay. Fairies were taking off from one runway and landing on the other. Halfway along the runways, fairies in orange overalls were holding small orange bats that looked like Ping-Pong paddles and waving them to the incoming flyers.

"Toots, when I get close to the runway," yelled Olive, "drop your feet down. As soon as they touch the ground, start running. Ready?"

"Ready!" Toots replied.

Toots thought this would be as easy as it sounded, but she soon learned otherwise. The ground rose up so quickly that it took her by surprise. She didn't even have time to start running. As Olive let go of her, her legs collapsed beneath her like wet straw. Luckily a small red-haired fairy close by caught Toots's hands and kept her upright until she came safely to a stop. In all the commotion Toots didn't notice the tiny white seed fall out of her pocket and bounce across the floor. Neither did anyone else.

The small red-haired fairy smiled at Toots. "That was really good for a first attempt," she said.

"Thank you," said Toots, blushing a little.

"You must be Toots," said the fairy. "I've heard a lot about—" The small fairy broke off, her eyes widening in horror. "Loose seed!" she cried, pointing to the runway.

Everyone stopped to look at the small white dot on the floor. The seed was turning yellow. A damp, oily stain appeared around it and spread rapidly. Toots felt in her pocket and realized with horror it was the seed that she'd picked up. Suddenly, Olive was at Toots's side. Before Toots could ask her what was happening, a deep voice silenced everyone in the room.

"Clear the runways!" it bellowed. Toots turned and saw the largest, most ferocious-looking fairy she had ever seen. She was twice as tall as Olive and twice as fat. Her eyebrows were thick and ran in one straight line across her face. "Everybody back!" she roared. "It's only one seed. We should be able to control it. Do not panic!"

All the fairies hurried to the edges of the room. Olive grabbed Toots by the arm and pulled her along. Within seconds the runways were clear.

The greasy circle around the seed darkened and grew bigger, until with a soft plop the seed sank into the ground and disappeared, like a stone in water. Everyone held their breath.

Just then a fairy flew into the cavern and veered toward the runways.

"Turn around, Madeleine!" the fairies cried. "Go back! Don't land, Maddy!" But it was too late.

With a great crack the dark circle split and a sharp green thorn shot out of the ground. It pierced the room, burying its dagger-like tip in the ceiling. Madeleine screamed as one of the thorn's sharp barbs caught in the handle of her bucket. It carried her up and pinned her against the ceiling. The lid on her bucket flapped open.

"Oh, no!" whispered Olive. "Please let that bucket be empty. Please, please, please!"

The thorn stopped growing, and Madeleine dangled helplessly. She steadied herself and the bucket at her belt and, for a moment, it seemed as though everything was going to be all right. But then the thorn jerked and jabbed itself farther into the ceiling. Madeleine rocked forward, and her bucket tipped over. Hundreds upon hundreds of small white seeds spilled out and skittered across the ground, bouncing like marbles on glass. It was a disaster.

"Red alert!" bellowed the huge fairy. "Everybody out! We have to seal this landing bay immediately!" She hit a large button on the wall, and an alarm began to wail.

Everyone rushed toward the big metal doors.

"Go that way!" shouted Olive, pushing Toots along with the crowd.

"Where are you going?" Toots cried.

"To help Maddy!" Olive sprang into the air and flew toward the fairy caught on the thorn, who was now in tears.

Toots hurried along with the fairies, but at the door she turned and looked back. Olive was near the ceiling, trying to free the trapped fairy. On the floor were hundreds of yellowing seeds. One by one the seeds disappeared into the ground. A moment later the thick green thorns sprouted up, one after another, driving their tips deep into the ceiling.

"Out of the way there!" bellowed the huge fairy at Toots. "This room has to be sealed. Step back!"

Toots wanted to say, "Wait for Olive!" but the words dried up in her mouth when she saw the huge fairy glowering down at her. Toots hurried through the doors.

From the corridor Toots watched for Olive and wished desperately there was something she could do to help. She stared at the thickening tangle of furzeweed in the landing bay and felt a chill run over her heart. She wasn't sure if she was imagining things, but it looked as though there was something hidden in the thorns. It was a face, or rather part of a face. A yellow eye as thin and cold as a crescent moon was staring back at her. Toots glanced at the crowd of fairies around her—no one else seemed to have noticed anything unusual. She peered back at the thorns. Now the hideous eye seemed to be laughing. Its pupil was as beady and black as a crab's, and it danced in the yellow slit. Beneath the eye a long, dark gash opened up where the mouth should have been. Toots shivered. She tried to look away but found that she couldn't. Unable to stop herself, she took a step toward it. She would have gone farther, but suddenly Olive was pushing through the thorns with Madeleine clinging to her back. The yellow eye and evil mouth rippled like a reflection in a pond and vanished.

Olive's face was blotched with pink, her helmet had fallen to the back of her head, and her eyes looked wild. Toots rushed to her.

"Thanks," said Olive as Toots helped her carry Madeleine through the doors.

"Come on, out of the way," bawled the big fairy. As soon as Olive, Toots, and Madeleine were clear, the huge fairy slammed the doors and slid the bolts in place.

"I'm so sorry," sobbed Madeleine.

"Humph! No use crying over it now, is there?" was all the huge fairy would say as she placed two sturdy bars across the doors and banged them into place. "Landing bay number three is now out of service," she croaked. She blew her nose noisily, then added, "Nothing more to see here. Everyone back to their classrooms and/or offices on the double."

"Who is that?" asked Toots in a whisper.

"Our wing commander. Wing Commander Lewis," replied Olive as she steered Toots up the corridor.

"If she's a wing commander, why is she so big?" asked Toots. Olive had said that a higher a fairy's ranking, the smaller she became.

"Sssshhh!" said Olive, lowering her voice. "She was once a group captain but lost her commission. A thing like that sets you back a long way."

"Oh," said Toots.

"The wing commander's wonderful," said Olive, "but be careful. She's not partial to humans—thinks they're more trouble than they're worth. She wouldn't have let me bring you here at all, but the group captain insisted." Olive glanced back over her shoulder. "The poor wing commander. That's the fourth landing bay we've lost to the furzeweed this week. At this rate all our exits, even the tiniest, most secret ones, will soon be sealed, and the furzeweed will trap us here forever."

"Olive," asked Toots, "why can't I see the furze-weed in the garden?"

"You could if you dug deep into the ground," replied Olive as she hurried ahead of Toots. "Unlike most plants, furzeweed grows down instead of up. It burrows deep into the earth and chokes a garden from beneath."

Toots shuddered.

"Come on," said Olive, giving her shoulder a friendly nudge. "We're not beaten yet. We've got to get to the group captain."

"Is she like the wing commander?" asked Toots a little nervously.

"Heavens, no," laughed Olive. "She's much sterner. Come on."

Toots gulped and followed her friend.

3 THE GROUP CAPTAIN

The pale green corridor was packed with bustling fairies, but Olive managed to move quickly, weaving through the crowd like a swift boat in a busy shipping lane. Toots had to trot to keep up.

As they went, Toots peeked into the rooms that lay on either side of the corridor. She caught only a fleeting glimpse of an intricately detailed map, a classroom blackboard that was covered in arrows and labeled WIND DIRECTIONS FOR APRIL, and a fascinating room where fairies were pushing little plants across a tabletop model of the garden. At last Olive stopped in front of a large door. Beside it was a window with a frosted sliding-glass hatch.

"Here we are," said Olive, straightening her flying suit and tucking her unruly hair into her helmet. "Ready?" she asked. Toots nodded, and Olive rapped smartly on the door.

The glass hatch instantly slid open and the wing commander's big red face appeared.

"Is that her?" she demanded, thrusting her chin at Toots. Toots shrank back against Olive.

"Yes, ma'am. This is Toots."

The wing commander scowled.

"Humph! Humans! Bring her in, then. And let's hope she's as good as you say."

The wing commander slid the hatch shut, and Olive had barely enough time to give Toots an encouraging smile and whisper, "Don't worry. Her bark's far worse than her bite," before the door flew open and the wing commander gruffly beckoned them in.

"The group captain's waiting for you," she said. "You know the way."

"Yes, thank you, ma'am. Come on, Toots." Olive led Toots through a small outer office to a door on the other side. Olive knocked, opened it, and ushered Toots inside.

They entered a large, cozy room full of furniture and overflowing bookshelves. It was so crowded that there was hardly an inch of carpet to be seen. Most of the space was taken up by an enormous wooden desk covered in papers and books.

Standing on a stool by the desk with her nose buried in a book was the little red-haired fairy who had helped Toots in the landing bay. The fairy looked very young, almost too young to be a garden fairy. Toots wondered what she was doing in the group captain's office, looking through the group captain's things.

Olive coughed politely, and the little fairy looked up.

"Pardon me, ma'am," said Olive deferentially, "may I introduce Toots? Toots, this is our group captain."

"Oh . . . ," gasped Toots, opening and closing her mouth like a fish. How could someone so young be in charge of a whole squadron of fairies?

The group captain smiled and heartily shook Toots's hand. "Don't be fooled," she said with a wink, guessing the source of Toots's confusion. "I'm older than I look." There was a knock at the door, and the group captain looked up. "Yes, Wing Commander, what is it?"

"Thought you might like a spot of refreshment, ma'am," came the reply.

Toots turned and saw the wing commander enter the room, carrying a dainty tea tray in her huge hands.

"Ah, tea. Just the thing. Thank you, Wing Commander Lewis," said the little fairy. The smile fell from her face and her eyes grew serious. "What's the latest report?" she asked.

The wing commander stood with her hands

behind her back and cleared her throat.

"Ehem . . . Landing bay number three is now confirmed inoperative, ma'am."

The group captain shook her head, reached over to a map on the desk, and drew a large red X by the foot of the horse chestnut tree. She rapped her knuckles on the desk and looked up. "Lewis, please stay while I brief Toots on the situation."

"Very good, ma'am," replied the wing commander, looking down her nose at Toots. Toots felt a little uneasy and inched closer to Olive. The wing commander sniffed and looked away.

The group captain sat on the edge of her desk with her legs dangling. She motioned for Olive and Toots to make themselves comfortable, then clasped her tiny hands together on her lap.

"Well, Toots," began the group captain, "we've heard all about your bravery in the Upside-Down House and how your ingenuity saved the house from the evil forces of Jack Frost."

Toots blushed. That episode had had many twists and turns, and she couldn't think of it without a twinge of shame. She would have liked to explain, but the group captain went on.

"Today, Toots, you saw the damage the thorny furzeweed can cause. You saw how it invades and destroys the garden by burrowing down and choking the soil. If the furzeweed is allowed to continue taking over the garden, all the plants, and even the horse chestnut tree, will die."

"The horse chestnut tree?" Toots interrupted. "But Mr. Phelps said that it was already dead. He's going to chop it down."

"What?" the wing commander bellowed, spilling her tea. "What do you mean? Who's going to chop it down?"

"Mr. Phelps, the tree surgeon," replied Toots.

"Oh, no!" gasped Olive. "When are they going to chop it down?"

"Tomorrow afternoon," said Toots, feeling very awkward.

"Hah!" barked the wing commander, mopping up the spilled tea with her handkerchief. "How typical of humans! The tree isn't even dead, and they want to cut it down."

"We don't *want* to," protested Toots. "But Mr. Phelps says if it isn't cut down, the whole garden will die."

"The tree's not the problem!" snapped the wing commander with such ferocity that Toots rocked back against Olive.

"Thank you, Wing Commander," said the group captain, holding up her hand. She turned back to Toots. "Tomorrow, you say?" The group captain looked thoughtful. "Then there's even less time than we thought." She was silent for a moment; then she said, "I'm afraid the furzeweed isn't our only problem. If it was, we wouldn't need help so desperately. No, I'm afraid our problem is far greater. You see, something is making the furzeweed stronger than it should be. Something is using it to take over and destroy the garden."

Olive's hands flew up to her mouth. "I was right!" she gasped.

The group captain nodded. "Yes, Olive, I'm afraid you were. I'm almost certain we have a waspgnat in the garden, and unless we can find and defeat it, the garden will die."

"What's a waspgnat?" asked Toots in a whisper. "How did it get here?"

The three fairies looked at each other.

"Well . . . ," began Olive in a halting voice, "a waspgnat is a garden fairy's greatest fear."

"No garden in living memory has ever survived one," said the wing commander. "Some say that they are—" But she was cut short as a book fell to the floor with a resounding bang.

The group captain hopped down from the desk.

"Now, now, Wing Commander, never mind about that," she said, bending down to pick up the fallen book.

"I've never even heard of a waspgnat," said Toots.

"Well, it's not the sort of thing they teach in your schools," said Olive kindly. "Hardly any humans know about them, even though you don't have to be upside down to see them, the way you do with fairies."

"But how can it destroy the garden?" asked Toots.

"Ah, that's the terrible thing," said the group captain. "As soon as a waspgnat invades a garden, most of the creatures and insects leave. Spring will not come. Plants and trees wither and die. Any creatures who do not leave begin to behave contrary to their nature. Ants will not work, bees will not buzz, worms will not wriggle. Sometimes the influence of the waspgnat spreads so far that insects start to talk and give themselves names and airs and graces. By then the waspgnat has a very strong hold indeed."

"What do they look like?" asked Toots.

Olive shook her head. "No one knows, because no one has ever seen one and lived to tell the tale. A waspgnat devours its prisoners and turns them into wraiths, and wraiths can't speak."

The group captain quickly leafed through the pages of a book on her desk. "It says here that waspgnats are 'devilishly hard to find. They can roam all over the garden and hide anywhere. Once a garden has a waspgnat, there's very little hope at all.'"

"I knew of a garden that had a waspgnat." Toots jumped. She had almost forgotten that the wing commander was in the room. "No one could do anything to stop it," said the big fairy sadly. "It was using nettles then, not furzeweed. The whole garden was soon all nettles. That was a very unhappy time. So many fairies lost. It was a very unhappy . . ." The wing commander stopped and blew her nose noisily.

"We won't let that happen here," said the group captain kindly. "Toots is our last chance. If she can't help us, we'll leave immediately. We won't let any of our fairies become wraiths, I promise."

"But if you lose the garden," protested the wing commander, "they'll never give you another."

"I know," the group captain replied. She turned to Toots and looked her straight in the eye. "Will you help us?"

"Yes," answered Toots. "What do you want me to do?"

The group captain looked at her steadily.

"I want you to find a way to defeat the waspgnat," she said.

Toots looked from the group captain to the wing commander to Olive, then turned her eyes to the floor. How could they expect her to do that? How could anyone expect her to know how to defeat something she hadn't even known existed until a few moments ago? The group commander crouched down in front of Toots and looked her in the eye.

"Toots, you are the only one who can save the garden. That's why Olive brought you here. We have to get to the root of the problem. Do you understand?"

Toots tried to think. She didn't want to let the garden fairies down, but her mind was a blank. She had absolutely no idea how she was supposed to defeat the waspgnat. She didn't even know where to begin.

Toots shook her head. "I can't . . . ," she began.

"Giving up already, is she?" muttered the wing commander.

Toots sat up. "No. No, I'm not giving up," she said. She racked her brains. She knew she wasn't stupid, but she couldn't think of anything. Then she had an idea. It wasn't the idea that she was searching for, but it was an idea.

"I think . . . ," she began quietly. The three fairies leaned in close to hear. "I think I might be able to think of something if I had a little time."

The wing commander threw up her hands. "Time is the one thing we don't have," she groaned.

"Please listen," implored Toots. "I'm sorry I can't think of something right now. But if I go home, I might be able to find something in one of my father's books. Or perhaps I could ask him for help."

"She has a point," said the group captain. "It's not fair of us to put Toots on the spot like this. I suppose it wouldn't do any harm to wait for just one night. We'll still have time to move out in the morning if there's no other choice. But hopefully Toots will have found the solution by then." The group captain put an encouraging hand on Toots's shoulder. "Brown, please take Toots home now. We'll see you tomorrow, Toots, bright and early as you can."

"I can be here by half past eight," said Toots. Mrs. Willets would no doubt spend the whole day in front of the television and would never miss her.

"Very good," said the group captain. And with that she returned to the book on her desk and was soon lost in thought.

"You'll have to use landing bay number five," said the wing commander as Olive led Toots to the door. "It's one of the few still operational."

As Toots passed, the wing commander sniffed and looked down her nose at her again. Toots hurried past with her head down. *She really doesn't like me,* thought Toots.

4 The Search for an Idea

Landing bay number five was much smaller than number three, and four times as crowded. The air was thick with fairies landing and taking off, and all of them looked exhausted. A number of fairies were climbing ladders and emptying buckets full of seeds into huge metal drums, some of which bore bright paper labels. Toots recognized the labels. The drums were old tomato soup and baked bean cans. She was amazed at how big they were.

I must be really tiny, she thought.

"Right, Toots," said Olive. "Get ready to start running. Here we go. Now . . . run!"

Toots ran. Behind her she could hear Olive's thunderous footsteps and then her flapping wings. Then Olive's arms looped round her middle and they were flying toward a dark tunnel.

This tunnel veered sharply down. Toots soon realized it led to the grate over the backyard drain.

She could see the thick iron bars across the end of the tunnel, and beyond them the sky. The space between the bars looked dangerously narrow. The other fairies slipped through easily, but they were flying solo. How was Olive going to fit through with Toots?

"Breathe in," Olive yelled as they sped toward the narrow exit.

Toots closed her eyes and held on tight as Olive twisted sharply to the left. She heard the iron grating whistle by, then felt the fresh air on her face. She opened her eyes and breathed a sigh of relief. They'd made it. They were flying down toward the sky.

The afternoon had gone and the sun was setting. Olive carried Toots beneath the tops of the rose-bushes and swooped down past the sundial. The light bounced off the pond and golden ripples danced along the fence. Far below them in the sky, a solitary raven flew in lazy circles.

"Shall I leave you where I found you?" asked Olive, banking round toward the swing.

Toots was about to answer yes when the back door opened and Mrs. Willets appeared, her hands on her hips.

"Charlotte? Charlotte?" she called. Her voice was as loud as thunder to Toots's tiny ears, and the words were distorted and strange. "Time to come in. Your dad's home." Mrs. Willets stepped out into the garden, looking puzzled. Binky trotted at her heels and barked at the empty garden.

"You can't drop me by the swing, not with her standing there," said Toots. "Can you take me inside the house?"

Olive changed direction and flew toward the open door, but just as they reached it, Toots's father came out. "Where's Toots?" he asked anxiously when he saw Mrs. Willets standing in the garden alone. His voice too was loud and distorted.

Olive quickly veered to the right and flew down the side of the house.

"Look, my bedroom window's open!" cried Toots. "Quick, fly in there!"

Toots's father called for her, a trace of uneasiness in his voice.

"Hurry," she insisted. "I don't want him to think I'm missing."

Olive swiftly flew in through the window and landed on the underside of the dressing table. Almost immediately the dressing table began to shrink beneath her feet.

"I'll wait for you by the swing tomorrow morning," called Olive. She gave Toots a snappy salute, then flapped her wings and made ready to fly away.

"Olive, wait!" cried Toots. "Won't I just forget you like before? How can I remember your problem if I can't remember you?"

Olive's mouth dropped open. "That's a very good point," she said, her voice now sounding squeaky and small. "Here, catch." She unfastened her bucket from her belt and threw it up to Toots. "As long as you touch something from the Upside-Down World, you'll remember us. Don't lose it, whatever you do."

"I won't!" cried Toots as she caught the bucket. It was now the size of a thimble. She slipped it on her little finger and felt it tighten as she grew. But soon her finger became too big, and the bucket popped off and bounced against the underside of the dressing table. Toots picked it up and put it in her pocket, not realizing that she'd no longer be touching the bucket. Immediately all thoughts of Olive and the Upside-Down Garden began to fade, but so slowly that Toots didn't even notice.

Her feet soon covered almost half of the underside of the dressing table. There wasn't much room left for her to grow. Toots reached up and laid her hands flat against the floor. Just at that moment, her gravity switched back to normal. Toots fell to the floor and found that she was trapped beneath the dressing table. Her head was scrunched up against the carpet, her knees were bent against her chest, and her feet were caught against the table. She was stuck fast. She couldn't even shout.

"Help!" she muttered through gritted teeth.

A moment later her bedroom door flew open, and
Binky rushed in. He pounced on Toots, barking with
joy and licking her face and ears. Toots was defense-
less, and even if she'd wanted to, she couldn't have
pushed him away.

"Help!" Toots yelped, trying to worm away from
Binky's smelly dog-breath kisses.

"Toots! How on earth did you get yourself stuck
like that?" cried her father as he rushed into the
room and pulled Binky away.

"Oh, Charlotte, you did give us a scare," puffed
Mrs. Willets as she gained the top of the stairs and
entered the room.

"I was just playing," said Toots as her father lifted
the dressing table. Toots crawled out and got up.

"We thought you'd run away to join the army or
something," said her father, laughing.

"What a relief," gasped Mrs. Willets as she
fastened Binky's lead to his collar. "I'll be going,
then," she said. "See you tomorrow." She waddled
off down the steps, dragging the reluctant dog
behind her.

"You looked pretty funny down there," said
Toots's dad. "Come on, I've brought fish and chips
for supper."

"And mushy peas?"

"Of course. And I got extra in case you wanted to
run across the road and invite Jemma."

"Er . . . no, she's probably already eaten," Toots answered without looking at him. "I'll set the table," she said as she headed down the stairs.

As she took knives and forks from the drawer, she thought about Jemma. Maybe going across the road with a peace offering of fish and chips would be the right thing to do. She chewed her lip and thought about it. No, she decided. She didn't want to see Jemma or try to be friends with her again. Suddenly, the back door blew open and banged against the sink. Toots jumped and hurried to close it, but as she pushed it shut, she stopped and listened. There it was again, that horrible mocking laughter. Toots shook her head and closed the door firmly.

As she sat down to eat her supper, Toots had the strangest feeling that there was something she'd forgotten. She sprinkled vinegar on the battered fish on her plate, then loaded up her fork with chips, fish, and peas. It was her favorite meal, and it was so delicious that with the first mouthful everything else in the world disappeared.

They'd almost finished their supper when Toots's dad said, "Mrs. Willets asked me if we could look after Binky for the weekend. I said yes, is that all right?"

"Yes," answered Toots, but she wasn't really

listening. The nagging feeling had returned. Some-thing told her that whatever it was she'd forgotten, it was important. She shook her head again. *If it was important*, she thought, *it'll come back to me sooner or later.* Then she did her best not to worry about it at all.

5 A Secret Mission

When she woke up, the nagging feeling was much fainter. Now it was just as though she'd had a dream that she couldn't quite recall.

She sat up and stretched. Then she got out of bed, yanked a T-shirt over her head, and climbed into her jeans. Yawning, she started to tuck her T-shirt in, but because she was still half-asleep she dopily tucked it into her pocket instead of her waistband. As she did, her finger hit against the miniature bucket that was caught in the seam of her pocket.

"No!" she cried as everything she was supposed to have done flooded back to her. "Olive! The fairies! Oh, no!"

She looked at the alarm clock. It was eight thirty-five. Not only had she failed to come up with an idea to help save the garden, she'd also overslept. With one hand in her pocket so she wouldn't forget again, she dropped to her knees and put the top of her head on the floor.

"Olive?" she cried, looking everywhere frantically. "Olive?" Then she remembered. *The swing!*

Toots ran downstairs. She slowed her steps as she
went past the living room, where Mrs. Willets was
already settled on the sofa, then ran through the
kitchen, stopping only to pick up the pack of cheese-
and-pickle sandwiches that Mrs. Willets had made
for her. She stuffed the pack in her other pocket,
then hurried outside.

As she ran across the patio, she tried to come up
with an answer to the fairies' problem. She was cross
with herself for forgetting, and now she couldn't
think of anything.

Toots reached the swing and leaned over it. There
was Olive waiting for her, just as she'd said she'd be.

"I'm sorry I'm late," whispered Toots.

"Important thing is that you're here," boomed
Olive through the megaphone. "I was worried you'd
forgotten all about us."

"Oh, no," said Toots, not wanting to admit the
awful truth.

"Hang on, I'll come and get you," said Olive as
she flew up and wrapped the cobweb rope about
Toots's wrist.

While she was shrinking, Toots tried to think of
an answer.

Come on, she told herself, *it can't be that hard.* But
it was. Toots went over everything that had been said

in the group captain's office, hoping that would give her a clue, but what had they really told her? That this thing called a waspgnat, whatever that was, would destroy the garden and that Toots was the only one who could find it and get rid of it. But how was she supposed to do that?

Toots thought and thought, but the only other thing she could remember clearly was the way the wing commander had looked down her nose at her. How would the wing commander look when she found out that Toots didn't know what to do? Toots trembled just thinking about it.

All around her the wind shrieked and laughed, but Toots barely heard it.

Then Toots noticed something pressing against her leg. She looked down and saw a lump in her pocket. Toots was puzzled at first but then remembered. *The bucket!* She let go of the swing with one hand and pulled Olive's pail from her pocket. She quickly regained her grip on the swing and tried to direct her thoughts back to the problem at hand. She needed an answer and she needed one fast.

By the time I get to the bottom of the swing, I'll have thought of something, she told herself.

But she hadn't thought of anything when Olive helped her onto the underside of the seat and took the bucket from her.

I'll have it by the time we set off flying. But as Olive lifted her into the air, her mind was still empty.

I'll know when we get inside the Upside-Down Garden, she assured herself. But at the landing bay it was the same story. Nothing, nothing, nothing.

Toots's face burned as Olive led her through the crowd of fairies in the landing bay. She felt as though everyone was watching her. She followed Olive up the long corridor in silence. *They'll have to pack all this up soon,* she thought as they passed the classrooms. *They'll have to leave this afternoon.*

The wing commander was pacing back and forth outside the group captain's office. When she saw Olive and Toots, she stopped and scowled. Her expression seemed to say—well? But she didn't ask. She just opened the door and ushered them in.

The group captain smiled warmly at Toots. And Toots tried to smile back but found that she couldn't. Her mouth just wobbled. It was all too much for her. "I'm sorry," she said, burying her face in her hands and bursting into tears. "I tried and tried and tried, but I couldn't think . . ."

Olive helped her to a chair, and the group captain handed her a tissue. Gently, she said, "And your father? Did he have any ideas?"

Toots looked up miserably. "I didn't get the chance to ask him. I forgot about the bucket and then I forgot about everything."

The group captain sighed and smiled sadly. "That happens," she said, and because she wasn't angry Toots felt even worse.

"Doesn't she realize the situation!" said the wing commander. "The waspgnat is extremely active. It's three times stronger than it was. If she—"

The group captain looked sharply at the wing commander. The wing commander tried to hold her tongue but couldn't help adding, "I knew we should never have relied on a human."

Once again Toots buried her face in her hands. The group captain gently pulled them away.

"I think Olive had better take you home, Toots," she said, helping her to her feet. "Don't be hard on yourself. It was never an easy task."

She turned to the wing commander. "Lewis, see that all units are packed and ready to evacuate by late this afternoon. We'll use landing bay number one. Tell the cadets I want no heroics. No one is to search for the waspgnat and fight it on their own. The waspgnat is too strong. I cannot afford to have any of my fairies devoured and turned into wraiths."

The huge fairy sniffed loudly. Then, throwing Toots a terrible, blood-jellifying look, she turned smartly on her heel and headed for the door. When she reached it, she turned back and saluted. "Operation Clear Out is now under way, ma'am," she said. And then she was gone.

Olive and Toots followed her out.

"I'm so sorry, Olive," said Toots, her voice faltering. "I've let you down."

Olive put a fat arm about Toots's shoulders and guided her down the hall. "Shush. Don't worry," she said softly. "That never does any good." The fairy gave her a squeeze. "Come on, let's get you home."

All along the corridor, fairies were already rushing about, packing boxes and loading them onto trolleys.

"What will happen to you when you leave?" asked Toots. "Where will you go?"

"Oh, we'll be homeless fairies," answered Olive sadly. "A garden squadron without a garden. I suppose we'll be split up and reassigned to other gardens. All except the group captain, of course. She'll be demoted and never be put in charge of another garden. She has to take the responsibility for there being a waspgnat in this one."

"Oh," said Toots, who couldn't think of anything more useful to say.

Up ahead a crowd of fairies were busy packing. Fairies on ladders were taking down pictures from the walls and unscrewing light fittings, while others were packing books into baskets and rolling up maps. Olive quickened her pace and ploughed through the throng. Toots trotted after her.

Eventually, Olive turned down an empty corridor. "We'll take a shortcut through here to landing bay number five," she said as she marched ahead.

Toots followed, but they hadn't gone far when a door on their right opened just a crack.

"Brown," whispered a voice from within. Olive and Toots stopped. The room beyond was dark and shadowy. "Brown," came the voice again. "Come in here. Leave the human where she is."

"Toots, wait here for me," said Olive as she slipped inside. Toots peered in and saw the wing commander's large face half-hidden in the shadows.

The wing commander? Toots thought. *What does she want with Olive?*

Then the darkness swallowed Olive up, and the door closed behind her. But the door didn't click shut and, as Toots watched, it swung open a little way.

"I need your help, Brown," Toots heard the wing commander say. "You trust me, don't you?"

"Yes, ma'am," replied Olive.

"The group captain doesn't know I'm talking to you," whispered the wing commander. "And she mustn't know. Do you understand?"

"I think so, ma'am," said Olive.

Toots frowned. *What are they talking about?* she wondered.

"Everyone thinks no fairy has faced a waspgnat and survived to tell the tale, but I know of one fairy who did," the wing commander said. "It happened a long time ago, in a garden that was dying just like ours. That fairy didn't save her garden, but she tried—oh, how she tried. When she returned, she told me, 'You must never let it get hold of your thoughts. If it does, it will turn you into a wraith.'"

"But what is it you want me to do?" asked Olive.

The wing commander spoke quickly, as though the words themselves were dangerous.

"It will be difficult," she told Olive, "and incredibly dangerous. I want you to hunt down the waspgnat and steal its most precious possession."

"What is that?" asked Olive in a trembling voice.

"Shush," whispered the wing commander. "Always remember that the waspgnat will be listening for your thoughts. Never repeat what I am going to tell you. Don't even think it, or you'll give the game away."

The wing commander was silent for a moment, then went on.

"Have you never heard of the waspgnat's olm?"

"No," whispered Olive.

"The olm is a purple stone that the waspgnat holds in its chest. As the waspgnat increases in strength, the olm grows bigger. It is the secret of the waspgnat's power. That is what you must steal.

"But just stealing the olm does not kill the waspgnat. Once you have the stone, you must find a way to destroy it, and destroy it quickly. If you're not quick enough, the waspgnat will bury itself deep in the garden and start to grow another olm.

"Don't look so worried," continued the wing commander in a gentle voice. "We are lucky. We have one advantage. The waspgnat has no idea that any fairy knows about the secret of its power. It will not know that you are seeking the olm. As long as we have this advantage, we have a chance. That is why you must not breathe a word or even think about your mission beyond this room.

"Olive, you are the best cadet I have. You're the only one I can send. You have a strong mind, and that's your best, your only, defense. Will you go?"

"Can I take Toots with me?" asked Olive.

"No," replied the wing commander. "You must send her home."

Toots flinched. Why did the wing commander dislike her so?

"I'd go myself," continued the wing commander, "but the group captain would miss me. I have to depend on you, Olive. Will you do it?"

No, Olive, don't, Toots begged silently, all at once afraid that some harm would come to her friend.

"Yes, ma'am, I will," replied Olive.

"Good girl. You'd better start straightaway. You will have to go up through the worm tunnels. You'll have to let it catch you if you want to get close enough to steal the olm. And when it does, remember the only shield you'll have is your mind. Don't let it in. Don't let it learn why you have come. Tell it nothing. I have great faith in you, Olive. I know you won't let us down. Now go, quickly, and good luck."

Toots pretended to be engrossed in a map of the garden that was hanging on the wall, but she was worried about Olive. Why was the wing commander sending her on such a dangerous mission? The wing commander should go herself!

As Toots stared at the framed map, it was as though all its colors faded away and a shadow seeped in around the edges of her vision. Toots peered closer. What was that reflected in the glass? It looked like a pair of thin yellow eyes, laughing at her.

"Toots! Toots!" Olive shook her, and with a flash all the colors in the map returned and the lines came back into focus. "Are you all right? You're so pale." Olive put her hand against Toots's forehead, but Toots pulled away.

"I'm fine," she answered, but she wasn't. She felt rattled and strangely cross, and she didn't know why.

"Let's get you home," said Olive. "It's been a stressful morning. Your nerves are frayed. We'll go to the landing bay and find someone to fly you home."

"Aren't you going to take me?" asked Toots.

"I can't, I'm afraid," answered Olive, avoiding looking Toots in the eye.

Toots suddenly felt very scared for Olive. She wanted to offer to help her friend, but she couldn't say anything without admitting that she'd overheard Olive's conversation with the wing commander.

At landing bay number five Olive stopped and pointed at a fairy holding orange paddles. "Nancy there will find someone to take you home. Sorry to have to leave you high and dry like this Toots," she said in an overly cheery voice. Then suddenly her big chin wobbled. She gave Toots a quick hug, then let her go. "You'll be all right," she said. "Everyone here is a qualified flyer."

It was more than Toots could stand. She grabbed Olive's arm.

"Olive," she said urgently. "I know you're going to go after the—"

Olive clapped her hand over Toots's mouth. "Shsssh," she said, her eyes opening wide in alarm. Olive drew her to one side. "You mustn't think about that at all! Wipe it from your mind. Now please go home. You'll be much safer there."

Then Olive turned away and hurried down the corridor.

Toots looked at the fairy with the orange paddles and then at Olive hurrying away. She couldn't just leave and let Olive go on her strange and dangerous mission by herself. Olive was her friend, and friends were supposed to help each other, weren't they?

Without another thought Toots set off after Olive. She ran silently along the corridor, keeping far enough back that Olive wouldn't suspect that she was there.

6 THE WORM TUNNELS

Toots followed her friend down corridor after corridor until at last Olive stopped at a place where the painted plaster walls ended. Ahead of her lay an unlit, soil-lined tunnel, which disappeared up into the gloom. Olive paused by the last door in the corridor and reached into her bucket. She brought out a large ball of bright blue wool and tied one end to the doorknob. Then she took out a flashlight, flicked the switch, and pointed the broad yellow beam into the dark tunnel. Transparent grains of sand in the soil sparkled, and the tunnel glittered like a sidewalk at night. Olive followed the yellow beam into the passage, playing out the blue wool as she went.

Toots waited a moment and then followed. The air in the tunnel was damp and smelled richly of earth and mushrooms. Whenever Olive turned a corner, the light vanished with her, and Toots had to run her fingers along the blue wool to make sure she was going in the right direction. She was careful not to pull at the wool and give herself away.

It was warm in the earthy tunnel, warm and dark and interesting. The tunnel sloped up into the ground, and the higher they climbed, the warmer it became.

After some time the narrow tunnel opened into a chamber with three tunnels leading off it. Olive took the tunnel on the left and soon after turned to her right. There were several more turns to the left then another to the right until Toots felt utterly confused. Now she understood why Olive trailed the wool behind her. Without it, it would be easy to lose your way. If you got lost in this maze, you could stay lost forever, wandering round and round and never getting anywhere.

Suddenly, Olive switched off her flashlight and the dark crowded in.

"Oh!" cried Toots, instantly wishing that she hadn't made any noise. She cowered in the darkness, listening as footsteps approached. There was a click and suddenly the beam of the flashlight blinded her.

"Toots!" exclaimed Olive in a whisper. "What on earth are you doing? Why are you following me?"

"I want to help. Friends should help each other, shouldn't they?"

"Yes, but—" Olive smiled. "Well, Toots, I'm

actually glad you followed me. This place gives me the creeps!" Olive crouched down and looked at Toots very seriously. "If I take you with me, you'll have to be very quiet. And that means quiet inside your head as well as outside. If the waspgnat is close by, it will be able to hear your thoughts as easily as you can hear me now. Do you understand? You mustn't go wondering off."

"Don't you mean *wandering* off?" asked Toots.

"Yes," replied Olive, "but I mean don't go wondering off, too. The waspgnat could be anywhere. You must keep a good hold on your thoughts. You must forget everything you heard the wing commander say. Do you promise?"

"I've forgotten it all already," said Toots with a smile.

"Good girl," said Olive. She fished in her bucket, brought out another flashlight, and handed it to Toots. "Here."

Toots switched it on, and the walls sparkled. She gazed at the tunnel around her.

"Olive?"

"Yes?"

"If these are worm tunnels, what happens if we meet a worm? Will it eat us?"

Olive laughed. "No, these are their old tunnels. We took them over and made them bigger for when we need to climb deep into the garden. Don't worry about the worms. If we do meet one, they're very friendly and would happily let us pass by."

"Where exactly are we going?" asked Toots.

"To find the root of the problem" was all that Olive would say.

Toots followed Olive along the tunnel. As they walked, Toots began to hear someone singing. She stopped and listened.

"Keep up," whispered Olive, shining her light on Toots. "You must keep up."

"What's that singing?" Toots asked in a whisper.

Olive cocked her head to one side. "It's a sign of how bad things are up here," she said sadly. "Remember the group captain told you that when a you-know-what has a strong hold on a garden, the insects begin to behave strangely? Well, there you are. Whoever that is is probably lost in the worm tunnels."

"Shouldn't we try and help?"

Olive shook her head. "There's no point. We'd probably never find them, not if we searched for years. That's the terrible thing about these tunnels. They distort sound. You can never tell where anyone is. That poor soul could be shouting to you from two yards away or whispering from two hundred. You'd never know."

"If I got lost, you'd come and find me, wouldn't you?" asked Toots, feeling a little nervous.

"You're not going to get lost," replied Olive. "If you did, I'd never get you home in time for supper, so please keep up."

"The singing's stopped now," whispered Toots. "Perhaps they've found a way out."

"Perhaps," said Olive doubtfully as she set off again.

They tramped on and on until, at long last, Olive stopped and switched off her flashlight.

"Turn yours off, too," she said softly.

Toots did so and to her surprise found that the tunnel wasn't pitch-black anymore. Now it was filled with a gray light like the sky just before the sun comes up.

"There must be a dog hole up ahead," whispered Olive.

"A dog hole? Do you mean one of Binky's holes?"

Olive nodded. "That's right. We'll have to go carefully around that."

As they pressed on, the light became stronger, but it wasn't until they turned a sharp bend that they saw that the tunnel came to an abrupt end. At first it looked as though there was nothing but sunshine beyond the end of the tunnel, but as Olive's and Toots's eyes got accustomed to the light, they saw that the tunnel had been cut in half by the dog hole. On the other side of the hole they could see the continuation of the tunnel.

Toots stood as close to the end of the tunnel as she dared and peered over the edge. Looking up, she could see the rough-domed bottom of the hole perhaps twenty feet above them. Looking down through the hole to the world outside, she could see the broad trunk of the horse chestnut tree, its bare branches still covered in the white furzeweed seed heads. High in the branches the raven's nest swayed in the wind, and beyond this the sky was full of big white clouds. Toots leaned forward to see better and the ground crumbled beneath her feet. Olive pulled her back.

"Be careful," she said. "There's an overhang here. The earth could easily give way."

Olive stood with her hands on her hips and studied the dog hole.

"I'd fly you across, but with two of us there isn't enough room in the tunnel to flap my wings. They would catch on the ceiling." She crouched down and picked up a handful of the loose soil. "And this is too freshly turned to support you if you climbed around the edge." Olive stood up, dusting the soil from her hands and gazing up at the round bottom of the hole. "I know!" she said. She reached into her bucket and pulled out her coil of cobweb rope. She fastened a grappling hook to one end of it, then swung it up toward the bottom of the hole. The barbed points of the hook caught in the

71

earth. Olive pulled. The hook had caught around a root and it held fast.

"Do you think you can swing across?" asked Olive as she offered Toots the rope. Toots pulled on it. She wasn't sure. It felt sturdy enough, but what if it wasn't? What if she fell?

Toots took a deep breath. She had promised to help, and she wasn't going to give up now. She backed along the tunnel, wrapping the rope around her wrist. She'd done this hundreds of times in games at school, but at school there'd always been mats beneath her, not the endless sky.

Toots didn't want to think of that now. She tugged on the rope, then raised herself up on her toes and ran. The dog hole came up very fast, and suddenly she was whizzing across it. The sky passed in a flash, and in less than a second she was across.

Back on the other side Olive unwound a good length of the blue wool, put the rest of the ball in her pocket, then waited while Toots pushed the cobweb rope back to her. Olive caught it and swung across the hole with the wool trailing behind her. Red-faced and out of breath from the exertion, she landed beside Toots.

"Whooph! That wasn't too bad, was it?" she said cheerily, looking back at the strand of blue wool that ran across the hole. Then she took the cobweb rope in both hands and gave it a sharp jerk. The grappling hook released itself from the root, and the rope fell down. Toots gasped.

"Could that have happened when I was swinging on it?" she asked, horrified.

"Oh, no," said Olive. She quickly coiled the rope and dropped it back in her bucket; then she took the ball of wool from her pocket and began to unwind it as she walked. "Come along. No time to dilly-dally."

Fifty meters farther on they came to another dog hole. It looked as though they could cross this one in the same manner as the first, and Olive was about to fix the rope to the bottom of the hole when suddenly a *Woof!* as loud as thunder shook the ground beneath their feet.

Olive yanked Toots out of the way just in time, for a moment later Binky shoved his enormous brown head into the hole. He sniffed and snorted and sneezed and scrabbled to get as far in as he could. He barked again, and it was so loud that Toots thought her eardrums would explode.

"Quick!" cried Olive. "He doesn't want to hurt us, but he could cause an accident if he's not careful."

Olive pulled Toots back along the tunnel toward the first dog hole, but Binky was too quick for them. They heard him running along the grass beneath their feet. For Toots and Olive the distance between the holes was at least fifty yards, but for Binky it was less than one. When they got to the first dog hole, he was already waiting for them with his shiny wet nose blocking the entrance to the tunnel. His nose was so big that they could only see one nostril. It was as big as a wheel.

"Oh, Binky, stay there!" said Toots as she and Olive ran back to the second hole. But Binky liked this game and beat them to it. His nose was waiting for them when they got there.

"We'll have to think of something else," Olive said. From the way the earth was shaking, they could tell Binky was trying to dig deeper, and from the *thump thump thump* on the ground, they knew he was wagging his tail. Then Binky scrabbled faster, and with a determined wriggle he jammed his nose harder against the tunnel opening. At first he was very pleased about this, and Toots and Olive could hear his tail thumping even louder, but then he began to whimper.

"Oh, Binky. What's the matter?" cried Toots.

"He must have got his head stuck in the hole," said Olive, handing Toots the ball of wool and delving into her bucket. She pulled out the cobweb rope.

"Wait here," she said. "I'm going to fly down and help him. I'll be back in a minute." Then, leaving Toots holding the ball of wool, she ran back to the first dog hole.

Toots gently patted Binky's nose. Binky whimpered. "Shush, boy," said Toots gently. "Shush."

Binky sniffed. His nostrils looked like two black tunnels in the mountain of his nose. Toots jumped. She shone her flashlight on Binky's nose. Two nostrils? A moment ago she had only been able to see one. Then it dawned on her. Olive was shrinking Binky and bringing him to the Upside-Down World. *That's one way to get him unstuck*, thought Toots. *But what will Binky make of all this?*

Binky was shrinking quickly and was soon small enough to shove his entire snout into the worm tunnel. Once there, he moved his head from side to side and stuck out his great pink tongue. Toots shrieked as Binky licked at her legs and knocked her over. She dropped the ball of wool as she fell. It rolled toward Binky, and he scooped it up with his tongue.

Binky chewed on the wool, then spat out the ball, but strands of wool were still caught around his teeth. Toots would have tried to untangle them, but suddenly Binky opened his enormous mouth wide and the tunnel filled with his stinky doggy breath. Toots shrank back. Even though she knew that this was just Binky, who in the real world didn't even reach as high as her knees, it was rather frightening to see his mottled, very pink gums and enormous sharp teeth up close.

Binky whimpered again, and as he moved his head, Toots saw that Olive was squeezing past him into the tunnel, patting his great neck as though he was a horse.

"Hold on, Binky," called Toots as he tried to back out of the worm tunnel. She stroked his nose to try to keep him steady. "You'll be all right in a minute," she said.

Olive was holding one end of the cobweb rope. The other end, Toots could see, was tied to Binky's collar.

"Grab hold of my belt," said Olive, "and be prepared to take Binky's weight. Hold on tight. This could get tricky." And she was right. At that exact moment Binky's gravity switched. With a loud *yelp* he suddenly fell out of the hole and disappeared from sight, dragging Olive and Toots all the way to the edge. The ball of blue wool rolled after Binky. Toots tried to stop it, but she was too late. It fell into the sky.

"Don't mind that now," puffed Olive. "We'll get it as soon as we have Binky safe."

Together Olive and Toots stuck their heels into the ground and held on to Binky's rope with all their strength. Luckily, Binky was quite small by this time. If he'd been his full size, he would have dragged them out of the hole and the three of them would have been lost forever, but he was getting smaller all the time. They just had to hold on until he became small enough for them to be able to pull him inside.

"I think we can try now," puffed Olive. "One, two, three, heave!" Toots gritted her teeth and pulled on Olive's belt. Olive gritted her teeth and pulled on the cobweb rope. Before long Binky was scrabbling over the edge of the tunnel. Toots was relieved to see that he was his usual size and came only to her knees. He bounded toward her.

"Down!" she laughed, holding up her hands. But Binky jumped up at her anyway. He knocked her down and tried his hardest to lick her face and ears. Then he jumped back, crouched, and barked once.

"Shush, shush, I know you're happy to see us," said Olive, making a great fuss of him. Binky wriggled like a gleeful eel as she patted his back and scratched his ears. "Now, shush. If you're not quiet, the waspgnat will find us, and we're not quite ready for that yet." To Toots's amazement, this had a most extraordinary effect.

Binky stopped barking, sat down obediently, and looked up at Olive as though waiting for her next command.

Olive untied the cobweb from Binky's collar, then carefully untangled the remains of the blue wool from between his teeth.

"Oh, dear, it looks like we've lost the rest of the ball," said Olive, holding up the frayed end of the wool. "He must have bitten through it when he was in the air." Toots paused for a moment to imagine that ball of wool falling forever into the endless sky. She shuddered.

"How will we find our way back now?" she asked.

"Well, we know how to get back to headquarters from here," said Olive, nodding at the line of blue wool disappearing into the tunnel behind them. "But we'll need to know how to get back to here from wherever we go. We'll have to improvise. If we make some kind of mark in the walls, something simple like this, look"—Olive dug four fingers into the soil of the right-hand wall, then pulled them out, leaving four perfect holes—"that'll show us how to get back. It's not as good as the wool, but it's better than nothing. Come on, let's get across here."

Binky's digging had made the dog hole even bigger, and now it seemed impossibly wide. To Toots's surprise, Olive clapped her hands gleefully.

"You've already done us a good turn, Binky," she said, giving Binky a pat on the back. "Clever dog. All your digging and scrabbling about has made enough room for me to fly you both across. One at a time, of course."

Olive picked Toots up and in an instant set her down on the far side of the hole; then she flew back for Binky. When all three were safely across, Olive made her mark in the wall, and they set off once more.

As soon as they moved away from the dog holes,

the worm tunnels began to lead up deeper into the earth. Soon it grew warm again, and the darkness became so complete that it seemed to swallow up the yellow beams of their flashlights. Every few feet Olive dug her fingers deep into the right-hand wall and Toots, following soon after, felt the holes just to make sure that she could find them.

"Here, Toots, look at this," whispered Olive as she stopped by a piece of old bottle glass embedded in the wall.

Olive rubbed the glass with her sleeve, then shone her flashlight through the frosted amber window. "This was a landing bay a very long time ago," she said. "Then for a while it was a storage area at the foot of the tree, but now . . ."

Toots pressed her face against the glass and saw acre upon acre of dark green thorns. "Furzeweed," she said.

"Look how dense it grows about the roots of the tree," said Olive, swiveling the light to the left. At first Toots couldn't even make out the huge roots of the horse chestnut tree for the thorns. Then the furzeweed suddenly moved and swept toward the window in a great wave. It crashed against the glass, and Toots leapt back.

"Oh, this horrible stuff!" said Olive. "It can look so harmless and then suddenly move as though it was an animal rather than a plant."

Olive turned to go, but something drew Toots back to the amber window. She held her flashlight to the glass and shone it into the far reaches of the cavern. Deep within the tangled thorns she saw the same evil, grinning face she'd thought she'd seen in the landing bay. The yellow eyes glinted and the smoking mouth was open wide in a horrible grin.

As Toots stared at the mesmerizing eyes, she grew cold all over and began to hear someone laughing. It was the same awful laugh she'd heard in the wind the night before, when the kitchen door blew open, only now the laughter was loud and strong. Toots felt suddenly angry, but she didn't know why. The reasons were all so muddled. She was angry with Jemma, with the wing commander for giving her those looks—she was even angry with Binky for losing the wool. Her head began to ache as though someone was squeezing it, and the warm amber glow of the window started to fade. The edges of her vision became crowded with gray shadows.

"Toots?" said Olive, pulling Toots away from the window. The laughter stopped abruptly. Toots rubbed her eyes. The gray shadows had gone.

"You have to be strong, Toots," Olive whispered. "Furzeweed this active is a sure sign that the waspgnat is close at hand. You mustn't let the waspgnat get hold of your thoughts."

Toots nodded and Binky growled softly as though

he understood as well. Then Olive beckoned to them to follow her along the dark tunnel.

Farther on the tunnels grew narrower, and they had to walk in single file. Olive led, Binky was second, and Toots brought up the rear. They climbed on and on, up deep into the earth.

As they traveled, Toots began to hear the strange singing again. Was it really an insect who had been affected by the waspgnat? Or was it a fairy lost in the tunnels? Toots shuddered and instinctively double-checked the marks that Olive was leaving in the wall. She didn't want to get lost.

The singing grew louder. Toots stopped and listened. She could almost hear the words. She shone her light into a tunnel on her left. It was empty, but she was sure that the singing was coming from there. It sounded so close.

Toots took one step into the empty tunnel and then another. Then she remembered that she was supposed to stay close to Olive and turned and ran back in the direction that Olive and Binky had gone. But when she rounded the next bend, there was only darkness ahead. Olive and Binky were nowhere to be seen, and there were no marks in the tunnel wall.

Toots ran on, desperately seeking the mark that Olive must have left. Where was it? Tears smarted in her eyes as she felt along the wall. The surface of the soil was smooth and unbroken. Suddenly, it occurred to her that Olive might have turned off somewhere, might have taken a different tunnel, one that Toots, in her frantic search, had missed.

Panic swept over her. She knew she shouldn't scream, but the need to call out to Olive was unbearable. Toots took a deep breath, but before she could shout, a hand closed over her mouth. A second hand quickly knocked her flashlight to the floor, and as the light went out, a third hand pulled her into the shadows.

7 ELIZABETH

Toots struggled, but the soft voice close to her ear whispered, "Shush. Keep quiet until the wind is past," and Toots felt her fear melt away. She stopped struggling and waited in the darkness.

The wind the voice had spoken of came quickly. As the warm air rushed up through the tunnel, the darkness seemed to change. Perhaps it was just her eyes playing tricks, but Toots thought she could see ghostly shapes in the wind, wispy, smoky shapes that swirled through the tunnel. Each had faint, thin yellow eyes like slivers of lemon peel. The eyes darted here and there as though searching for something. Toots shrank back against the wall.

The smoky wind quickly passed, leaving Toots and her mysterious captor alone in the tunnel. After a moment, the hands let her go. Toots immediately knelt down and, after a little fumbling, found her flashlight and switched it on.

She turned and was surprised to see what looked like an old lady cowering by the wall, shading her eyes.

"Too bright, too bright," whispered the old lady, waving away the flashlight. Toots politely pointed the beam at the floor, but as she did, she noticed that the old lady's hand was covered with bristly hairs. Not only that, but she had three other hands, one shading her eyes and two others pulling her tattered shawl around her shoulders. She also had two pairs of legs, and these were jointed in far too many places to be mistaken for a person's. Toots's mouth dropped open. The old lady wasn't an old lady at all.

It was some sort of insect, she realized. No, wait, it had eight limbs, and if it had eight limbs, then it was an arachnid, like a spider. Toots remembered pictures of mites she'd seen in a science book at school. It could be a mite, she supposed. Instead of a nose, the creature had a long proboscis. Stiff hairs stuck out of its hands and feet, and its body was covered by a swirling pattern like that of a fingerprint.

Toots stared at all this strangeness but didn't feel the least bit afraid. Perhaps it was because she couldn't quite believe what she was seeing, or because the creature was only half as big as Toots, or maybe it was because she could see tears caught in the hairs on the creature's face. For whatever reason, Toots knew that she had nothing to fear from this creature.

"What's wrong?" she asked, leaning forward.

The mite sniffed. It looked one way and then the other; then very softly it began to sing.

All of my children,
Poor hungry things,
Lost to their mother,
How my tears sting.

All of my children,
Poor hungry mites,
Lost and so frightened,
Alone in the night.

The song whispered down the tunnels, then echoed back far louder than the original.

"So that's why you sing!" Toots exclaimed. "You're looking for your children. How many do you have?"

"One hundred and seventy-two," sniffed the mite, barely moving its mouth. "You'd think that many would be easy to find, but I can't even find one of them."

The mite's black eyes shone with fresh tears, and it dabbed at them with a small handkerchief. It was only then that Toots noticed the wire muzzle around the mite's nose and mouth. It was wound so tightly that it dug right into its flesh. That was why the mite could barely open its mouth and could only speak in whispers. Toots winced. The muzzle looked painful.

"What's your name?" Toots asked.

"Elizabeth," came the whispered reply.

Toots reached out and very gently tried to unfasten the muzzle, but the wire was twisted too tight. She was about to try again, but the mite pulled away.

"It's no use," whispered Elizabeth as she bent down and picked up a satchel that lay by the wall. She looped the strap over her shoulder and set off at a shambling pace. After a few steps she paused and beckoned for Toots to follow.

Toots looked at the mite's kind face. *Perhaps,* she thought, *this mite will help me find Olive.* Toots knew that without the marks to follow she would soon be hopelessly and utterly lost. But she had to do something. Time was running out, and the fairies would be leaving the garden soon. Toots smiled at Elizabeth and together they set off along the tunnels.

As she followed the mite, Toots made a deep mark in the wall every five paces or so, the way that Olive had, but Toots used only three fingers. If Olive came to look for her, she'd know which way Toots had gone.

After many turns the mite stopped by a low door. She reached into her satchel and brought out a large bunch of keys. She carefully selected one and slotted it into the keyhole. Then she turned the key, opened the door, and slipped inside. Toots saw that beyond the door was a cavern crammed full of furzeweed. The thorns clacked together like angry knitting needles. The mite took no notice of the noise but, pulling a long, thin knife from her bag, began to lop off the tips of the nearest thorns and put them in her satchel. The furzeweed clacked louder. Toots jammed her fingers in her ears to block out the horrible sound. When Elizabeth's satchel was full, she slung it over her shoulder and came out, locking the door behind her. She beckoned to Toots, then set off once more along the tunnel. Now the weight of the thorns made the poor little mite list to one side as she walked.

They hadn't gone very far when Elizabeth stopped and held up her hand.

"Turn out your light," she whispered.

Toots turned off her flashlight and blinked at the sudden darkness. But it wasn't dark for long. Soon a glow as pale as moonlight began to spread through the tunnel, making the grains of sand in the soil sparkle like stars. Elizabeth pushed Toots back against the wall.

"Keep out of sight," she warned. "They'll be angry with me for staying out so long, but who knows what they'll do to you."

The light grew, but it was still muted and pearly like the light inside a shell. Two strange figures appeared around a bend in the tunnel.

"Elizabeth?" demanded one of them in a high, thin voice. "Elizabeth? Where are you? We can hear you."

"Eeeelizabeth," croaked the other in a voice even higher than the first. "Drat the creature, Sister, she should have been back with our treatment hours ago."

"She's probably still moping about her children."

"Her blasted children!"

"Her stinky children!"

"Her starving children!"

The two voices tittered. Toots, unable to restrain herself any longer, peeked around Elizabeth and saw two large, blindingly white creatures coming slowly up the tunnel.

They were dressed in long robes of heavy silk, and on their heads they wore high crowns of multi-colored feathers and lace. They both wore small, dark spectacles. One creature's were made of blue glass, and the other's of red. Their faces were as pudgy as uncooked dough. Their skin was dimply and looked as soft as marshmallow. It was so pale and shone so brightly that it created the pearly light that now illuminated the whole tunnel.

Toots had never seen anything like them as they glided grandly toward her, preceded by their mantle of light. Here were two more garden creatures that had been affected by the waspgnat. But who or what were they? Toots remembered what the group captain had said about how the creatures who remain in a garden with a waspgnat will behave contrary to their real nature. Ants will not work; bees will not buzz; worms will not wriggle. And she'd also said that sometimes the insects would start to talk and give themselves names and airs and graces.

Suddenly, one of them shrieked.

"Elizabeth! There you are. Where have you been?" The creature swooped down and poked Elizabeth with its dimpled finger.

"This is too, too bad," wailed the other. "You were supposed to be back hours ago. We can't afford to miss our treatment, you know. We don't want to dry up, do we?"

Toots peeked out from behind Elizabeth and watched the words pour out of the creatures' mean little mouths. For all their grand robes, they were behaving just like spoiled children.

"You know we don't like coming out into the tunnels to look for you," whined the first.

"It's so dirty and smelly down here," added the second. She shuddered, and her white flesh wobbled like jelly.

Suddenly, the first creature reached out and clamped a soft, doughy hand on Toots's arm.

"Sister, look!" squealed the creature as she held tight to Toots.

"Oooooh! Sister, what is it?" cried the other, shoving the mite out of the way.

"Elizabeth's picked up something nasty. Just look at its foul skin! It must have come from the garden. It's all red and ruddy and burnt to a cinder by that wicked, wicked sun. I'm lucky, Sister, that my skin has never suffered the effects of light."

"Yes, and I'm lucky, Sister, that mine never saw the moon because they say, and I believe it's true, that the moon can burn you almost as badly as the sun, and both are detrimental to complexions as beautiful as ours."

They bowed their heads and smiled at each other with strained sincerity. On closer inspection Toots could see that their skin wasn't as soft and glowing as it had first appeared. It was covered with hair-thin cracks like the glaze on a fine porcelain cup. Bits of skin were flaking at the edges of their cheeks and peeling away from their faces.

"Arghhh! Blanche," said the one with blue spectacles, "I'm starting to dry up. I can't move my mouth!"

"Oh, Palydia, me too," cried Blanche. "Elizabeth. *Elizabeth!* Quickly, we need our treatment now. *Now!* Oh, I can hardly move my mouth." Blanche lifted her hands to her mouth, dropping Toots's wrist to do so.

Elizabeth's eyes met Toots's. She cocked her head and whispered, "Run!"

"Don't let it get away, Sister!" shrieked Palydia. Blanche gasped and seized Toots firmly by the ear.

"Good work," said Palydia as best she could. Her skin was now so dry and cracked that it was nearly impossible for her to open her mouth. "Shall we take it with us?" asked Palydia. Blanche could only croak a reply.

Toots squealed as Blanche led her along the tunnel by her ear. A hundred questions raced through her mind. Why had she ever lost sight of Olive? Why on earth had she put her faith in a mite who wore a muzzle? And how was she going to get out of this dreadful situation? To make matters worse, Blanche pulled her along so quickly that she could no longer reach the wall to make a mark. How would Olive find her without the marks?

Little flakes of skin fluttered in the air behind the sisters as the strange procession wended its way through the dark tunnel.

8 PALYDIA AND BLANCHE

Eventually they stopped by a door in the tunnel wall. With a wince and a sob Palydia gingerly held out her flaking hand. Around her wrist was a heavy silver chain, and from this dangled a small, bright key. Ever so gently, Elizabeth took hold of the key and guided it toward the keyhole.

"Ow!" squealed Palydia, trying not to move her mouth. Large flakes of skin fluttered down from her wrist where the heavy chain chafed. "Oww," she groaned. "Why can't I just give her the key? Why do I have to wear it like this?"

"You know very well we can't have her running in and out all the time," replied Blanche through clenched teeth. "You know she can't be trusted. Now shut up and move closer to the door. You're making it take forever!"

"Ow, ow, ow!" wailed Palydia as Elizabeth fitted the key into the lock. "Be careful!"

As soon as Elizabeth had turned the key, Palydia pushed past her, completely forgetting that the key was still in the door. As the chain yanked against her wrist, Palydia ricocheted back into the tunnel and collided with her sister.

Blanche was not pleased.

Elizabeth intervened and quickly removed the key from the keyhole. Then she held the door wide open while Palydia dipped her feather-crowned head and disappeared inside. Dragging Toots by the ear, Blanche followed. Toots didn't want to go, but where her ear went she had to go, too.

The chamber they now entered was as different as could be from the dark, bare tunnel. It was splendid and strange. The walls and ceilings were hung with bright silks. Tall candles burned in elaborate candelabras. And all this splendor was reflected in many gold-framed mirrors on the walls. In the corners were two carved wooden screens that displayed pictures of tiny insects. Palydia immediately disappeared behind one of these, whimpering as she went. As soon as the door to the chamber was locked behind them, Blanche let go of Toots's ear and, with a muffled shriek, hurried behind the other screen.

Toots looked around. The strangest thing of all was that right in the middle of this fancy room stood two plain wooden tables. They didn't seem to belong there at all. At the far end of one table was a small cart on which stood a large, old-fashioned mincing machine with a huge wheel for grinding whatever was put into the funnel at the top.

Palydia soon appeared, wrapped in a fluffy pink bath towel. A moment later Blanche came out in a blue one.

With a great deal of difficulty the two sisters hoisted themselves onto the tables and lay back like languishing heroines. Elizabeth gently removed their spectacles. All around their eyes large pieces of skin were flaking away like peeling wallpaper. It looked painful.

"Hurry!" whined Blanche without moving her mouth.

"Hurreeeee!" screeched Palydia.

Elizabeth quickly transferred the furzeweed thorns from her satchel to the mincing machine and began to turn the handle. Soon great dollops of smoothly minced furzeweed dropped into a bowl at her feet.

"Make that thing you found help you," moaned one of the sisters.

"And hurry," groaned the other.

Elizabeth showed Toots how to turn the wheel in a continuous motion so that the minced thorn came out in one long, smooth dollop. Toots turned the wheel. It was more difficult than it looked. The wheel was stiff and the furzeweed tough to grind.

While Toots struggled to turn the wheel, Elizabeth rubbed each of the sisters all over with a rough washcloth. Soon the air was filled with large flakes of dried skin, not to mention the ear-piercing squeals of the sisters.

Once she'd rubbed each sister down, Elizabeth scooped up handfuls of minced furzeweed and smeared it over their rough white skin, piling it high like frosting on a cake.

"Ooooh, lovely, lovely," cooed Palydia, moving her mouth more easily. "I'll soon be as soft as a baby's bottom."

"Fa . . . fa . . . fa . . . fa . . . fabulous," giggled Blanche. "It's the most marvelous stuff for your skin. A little every day is good."

"But lots four times a day is better!" screamed Palydia. "Thank goodness there's enough of this stuff around to last us forever and ever."

"Thank goodness," echoed Blanche.

Toots had the hang of the mincing machine now. She added another thorn to the funnel. As she steadily turned the wheel, she watched the sisters get their unusual beauty treatment at the hands of the little mite. She was puzzled. Elizabeth was obviously a mite. But what were the sisters? She stared at their strange pale skin and pudgy bodies. And then suddenly she knew.

"Maggots!" she exclaimed. "You're maggots!"

Elizabeth looked at her quickly, her eyes full of warning.

"*Maggots?*" screamed one sister, sitting up sharply. "Did you say *maggots?*" A dollop of green goop slid off her large face. Toots trembled.

"We're not *maggots!*" cried the other, wiping furzeweed sludge from her eyes. "We are not nasty little grubs that turn into horrid flies. We are mag-go, *mag-go*. The T is silent. What a vile, ignorant little creature you are."

Elizabeth gently put her hands on the sisters' shoulders. "Now, now," she cooed as she settled them back down on the tables. "You don't want to ruin the treatment and have to wait for me to go and get more thorns, do you?"

The sisters did as Elizabeth suggested, but they were still annoyed with Toots.

"We'll make you pay for that cruel remark just as soon as we've finished our treatment," Blanche grumbled.

"And we'll muzzle you, too," snarled Palydia. "Elizabeth's been much better behaved since we muzzled her. She hasn't eaten any more of our treatment, has she, Blanche?"

"Which is quite as it should be," yawned Blanche. "Imagine if everyone learned the secret of our beauty treatment. Why, everyone would want some.

There'd be none left for us. And that would be terrible." Blanche yawned again.

"Oh, yes, indeed it would, Sister, indeed it would," said Palydia sleepily. "I think I'll take forty winks now," she added as she settled back on the table.

Blanche did the same, and Elizabeth slathered more green goop over their faces. When the sisters were completely covered, not one inch of their white skin showing through the creamy furzeweed, Elizabeth turned an hourglass over.

"Why do they cover themselves in furzeweed?" whispered Toots.

"Because it's the only thing that stops them from turning into chrysalises. They don't ever want to become flies."

"Why not?"

"They don't want to grow up. Change can be a frightening thing. Terrifying! Now all they care about is their appearance. But it's not their fault." Elizabeth's voice sank to a whisper. "Something in the garden is making them act this way."

Toots nodded. She knew exactly what Elizabeth meant. Toots would have told Elizabeth everything she knew, even about the face she'd seen in the thorns, but there wasn't time. The little mite steered Toots toward the door.

"Hurry now," said Elizabeth urgently. "They'll

wake as soon as the sand in the hourglass is gone. You mustn't be here."

Toots tried again to untwist the wire on Elizabeth's muzzle. "If you had some wire cutters, I could get it off for you," said Toots as she struggled with the knot.

"No," insisted Elizabeth, casting a nervous glance at the sleeping sisters. "There isn't time. If you are still here when they wake, they'll make you their slave, just like they did to me. You must go."

Toots twisted the wire on the muzzle and succeeded in loosening it a little.

"Thank you," whispered Elizabeth gratefully.

Toots tried the door. It was locked. "How will we get out?" she asked.

"Blanche keeps the real key, but I have this." Elizabeth pulled a long, thin bone key from her pocket and slotted it into the keyhole. She wiggled it about, but it wouldn't turn. Elizabeth pulled it out and began to whittle down the points on the key with a tiny file. Then she tried it again. Still nothing.

"When you get out, run as far from here as you can."

"But you're coming with me, aren't you?"

Tears started in Elizabeth's eyes. "I can't. For my children's sake, I can't." She nodded at the two on the tables. "They say they know where my babies are. They've promised to tell me, but they haven't yet."

"How cruel," said Toots.

The mite dabbed her eyes on her shawl. "Oh, that's not really their fault either," she said, trying to smile at Toots. "It's all these strange goings-on in the garden that make them this way."

Elizabeth stopped filing and blew on the key, then tried it in the lock again. She twisted and pulled and jiggled, but it still wouldn't turn.

"It ought to work," she said, throwing a worried glance at the hourglass. As the last few grains of sand trickled down, Elizabeth joggled the key and gave it one enormous twist. The lock clicked open at the very moment that the sisters opened their eyes.

"Elizabeth!" they both wailed, sitting up. "Elizabeth! Come and help us!"

"Go quickly," said Elizabeth, shoving Toots out the door with her thin, hairy arms.

Toots didn't move. She was staring at the sisters. The green goop had vanished. Their skin had absorbed every drop, and once again it glowed with a pearly light. It looked as soft and as white as summer clouds. All the dry flakiness had gone, but their eyes were red-rimmed and puffy. Toots realized it was the light from their own bodies that made their eyes smart. That was why they needed the colored spectacles.

"Go!" insisted Elizabeth, pushing her through the door, then closing it behind her. Toots landed with a *whumph* on the floor of the dark tunnel.

Remembering Elizabeth's instructions to run as far away as she could, Toots jumped to her feet, switched on her flashlight, and raced down the tunnels. She ran and ran until, believing herself incapable of running any farther, she collapsed on the ground with her heart pounding in her ears.

When she was finally able to sit up, she shone her flashlight over the smooth, dark walls, hoping to recognize something about the tunnel, but there was nothing. There were none of the marks that she or Olive had left. Toots sighed. She must be in another part of the worm tunnels. She was utterly, totally, and completely lost.

She leaned back and rested her head against the wall. She was tired and hungry and was wondering how long it would be before she'd eat again, when she remembered the sandwiches she'd brought from the house. She took them out of her pocket. They were squashed, but still edible. Toots quickly unwrapped one and bit into it.

Olive had probably been looking for her for ages and would be furious with her for getting lost. Perhaps she should have gone home when Olive insisted on it. She hadn't helped anyone. She'd only caused more trouble. Her father would be terribly worried when she didn't come home, and Mrs. Willets would be upset that Binky was missing. Toots sat holding the half-eaten sandwich and bitterly regretted that she hadn't listened to Olive.

Then a terrible thought, a distressing, nagging doubt, popped into her mind. What if Olive *wasn't* looking for her? Toots blinked. She knew it was ridiculous, but the doubt grew. What if the wing commander's secret mission was more important than searching for Toots? What if Olive had abandoned her?

Toots shook her head. Olive would never do that. Olive wouldn't leave her lost and alone in the tunnels, but . . .

Toots thought back to when she'd last seen Olive and Binky. They had disappeared awfully quickly. Had Olive left her on purpose? No. Toots couldn't believe that. Olive wouldn't leave her. Olive was a true friend—but then Toots had once thought that Jemma was a true friend, too.

As Toots thought and thought, the doubts raced through her mind, piling up one on top of another. Grayness crowded in around the edges of her vision. The colors in the opposite wall began to fade, but Toots didn't notice. Her thoughts raced on.

Now Toots could see it as clear as day. Olive wasn't her friend at all. Olive didn't care about her. She was just out to get some sort of promotion. That was why she was willing to risk her neck to steal the waspgnat's olm.

A shriek of laughter echoed triumphantly down the lonely tunnel. Toots sat bolt upright. It was the laugh she'd heard in the garden and in the tunnels, and all at once she knew without a doubt that this was the waspgnat's laugh.

Her blood grew icy cold. The waspgnat had heard her thoughts. It had used her to glean the information it needed. Toots hung her head. She'd gone and told the waspgnat the purpose of Olive's secret mission.

Toots groaned. Olive would never betray her or abandon her or put her in danger. But now Toots had done as much to Olive.

The laughter echoed again in the darkness. A warm wind began to race through the tunnel, and the air became thick with smoky gray shadows. Toots knew what they were now. They were the waspgnat's wraiths. It had sent them to find her! Toots staggered to her feet. Her legs felt like lead, but she had to get away from the awful laughter and the ghostly shapes. She switched off her flashlight and, still clutching the half-eaten sandwich, ran into the darkness as fast as she could, blindly feeling for any gaps in the walls that would lead her into new tunnels.

On and on she ran until her legs felt as weak as straw. She didn't notice exactly when she'd left the smoky wind and the horrible laughter far behind. She kept on running until she felt her lungs would burst; then she slowed and, gasping for breath, stopped to rest in the darkness.

For a while she couldn't hear anything but the *thump* of her heart. As she recovered her breath, she began to hear another sound behind her in the blackness. Something was coming quickly along the tunnel toward her. It made a scrabbling, scratching, snuffling sound. Toots knew she couldn't run anymore; she was too exhausted. Whatever it was, it was getting closer. Toots buried her face against her knees and held her breath, praying that it would miss her in the darkness. It didn't. Toots shrieked as it leapt on her shoulder and licked her ears, then scrabbled for the sandwich in her hand.

"*Woof!*"

Toots switched on her flashlight as relief flooded over her.

"Binky!" she cried as the happy, wriggling dog tried to eat the sandwich and lick her face at the same time. "You found me!"

"*Woof, woof.*"

"Shush," whispered Toots. "Good dog! You're a clever, clever boy."

chapter

9 THE TREE

When Binky had quite finished telling Toots how pleased he was to see her, and Toots had quite finished telling Binky what a smart and clever dog he was, Toots looked around hopefully. She expected to see Olive hurrying along the corridor at any moment, but no one came.

"Where's Olive?" she asked, but Binky just wagged his tail and stood with his tongue hanging out of the side of his mouth. Toots grew worried. What had happened to Olive? Perhaps she was lost in the worm tunnels, too. Perhaps she was waiting for Toots to come and find her. Toots jumped to her feet, and Binky bounced up beside her.

"Go seek," she told him. "Come on, Binky. Go seek Olive."

Binky seemed to understand and, with the closest thing to a whispered woof, he put his nose to the ground, circled twice round Toots, then set off.

"Good boy!" Toots said, chasing after him.

On they ran through the dark tunnels, but there was no sign of Olive. Toots was on the verge of despair when the beam of her flashlight struck a familiar mark in the right-hand wall. Her heart leapt. It was the imprint of Olive's four fingers! Now Toots raced ahead of Binky with her flashlight following the wall. Every few feet there was another of Olive's imprints pointing the way. Toots hurried on. Soon everything would be all right.

But as they turned the next corner, Toots's heart fell, for there in front of them was the second dog hole. Binky ran and stopped just short of it, then looked back over his shoulder at Toots and whimpered. Toots crouched down beside him and stroked him gently. Binky hadn't brought her to Olive; he had brought her home, or as near to home as he could bring her. She couldn't be angry with him about that. But this didn't help matters much. She still had to find Olive, and they still had to save the garden.

Toots sighed. They'd been following Olive's marks in the wrong direction, and that was why they'd led her back to the dog hole. Then she realized something and jumped up. They couldn't be the same marks. Olive's original marks had been in the right-hand wall, but only when they'd been headed the other way. Toots looked at the other wall. There were Olive's original marks. It could only mean one thing: Olive had come back this way! She must have crossed the dog hole and returned to headquarters, probably to form a search party to look for Toots.

Toots felt sure of it. She shone her light into the shadows on the other side of the hole to see if she could see any sign of her friend. That was when she saw Olive's flashlight lying abandoned on the ground. All around it the soil had been churned up. It looked as though there'd been a struggle!

"Something's happened to Olive," she told Binky. "Perhaps she was captured by the waspgnat."

If that was the case, Toots would have to do for Olive what Olive had been trying to do for her. She would have to go back to headquarters and get help. It didn't matter if the wing commander shouted at her; she had to help Olive.

Toots studied the wide hole in front of her. How was she going to get across? There was no ledge around it, and the dirt was too loose to provide any footholds. And even supposing she made it, how would Binky get across?

There had to be a way. Toots studied the inside of the dog hole and saw a twisted root embedded in the wall not too far away. She stretched over as far as she dared and gently scraped the dirt away from it. When she had removed as much soil as she could, she slipped her fingers beneath the root and pulled. It was only just beneath the surface and unraveled easily from the wall. It stopped unraveling close to the bottom of the hole, which, if she judged it right, would give her just enough of an angle to be able to swing across. It wouldn't be easy, but it was worth a try.

The root was old and brown and now much longer than she needed. It seemed strong, but would it be strong enough to carry her weight to the other side? Holding it in both hands, she pulled with all her might. Behind her Binky latched on to the root with his teeth and pulled as well. The root held.

"It'll do," Toots declared.

Even though Olive was missing, Toots was beginning to feel a little better about the whole situation. At least now she knew where she was. All she had to do was get across the two dog holes, then follow the blue wool back to headquarters and form a rescue party. She was sure that with the help of the other fairies she'd soon be able to find Olive. For the first time Toots felt that she was getting somewhere. If she could just get across the dog holes, everything would be all right.

She held Binky under one arm and clutched the root with her free hand. Then, counting to three, she launched herself and Binky over the edge. The long, ragged tip of the root waggled around the rim of the hole as they swung.

Toots soon found she had misjudged the distance.

She was only just able to reach the tunnel with her feet and balance precariously on the edge, still clinging to the root. She would have to try to swing at the tunnel again.

"Can you jump into the tunnel, Bink?" she asked. Binky could. He scrambled over Toots and leapt to the ground. Then he stood there, barking encouragement. Toots lowered herself a little farther down the root, then pushed off and began to swing back and forth. With each swing she came just a bit closer to the tunnel, but then a dark shadow passed over the dog hole and a loud screech drowned out Binky's barks.

"*Kronk!*"

Toots looked down and saw an enormous raven staring at the end of the root with an unmistakable gleam in his bright eye.

Oh, no! He thinks the root's a worm! thought Toots as she swung back toward the tunnel. But before she could even try to touch the side with her feet, the raven had grabbed the end of the root in his beak and was pulling on it ferociously.

"Let go!" Toots screamed. "Go away!"

But the raven, intent only on his dinner, gave one more ferocious tug. There was a sudden and terrible ripping sound, and the root came out of the earth with such a jolt that Toots couldn't hold on. She screamed as she fell toward the clouds.

Binky barked after her.

"*Kronk!*" cawed the raven, finding he'd caught nothing but a dry, dead root.

Toots's fall was fast but surprisingly short. It was over before she really had time to realize that she was falling. Lucky for her, the raven's messy nest lay directly in her path. Toots crashed into the bottom of it and lay there breathless, staring up at the garden.

She ran her hand through the deep layer of white, feathery seed heads that covered the underside of the raven's nest. Most of them had their tiny white seeds attached. Now that the fairies were leaving the garden, the furzeweed would soon take over.

Toots gazed up at the tree's thick trunk and sprawling roots far above her and sighed. Now she was even further from finding Olive. It was so frustrating! Toots shook herself. She had to get to the fairies before they left the garden for good. Time was running out, not only for Olive, but for the horse chestnut tree as well. Mr. Phelps had promised to come around at four o'clock that afternoon, and it had to be after lunchtime already. What could she do?

Toots squinted up at the enormous tree. Perhaps if she climbed up to the roots, she could find a way back into the garden fairies' headquarters. She got to her feet and, remembering how her father always said that "even the longest journey starts with a single step," she set off along the underside of the branch. It was as wide as a freeway and rose up like a steep hill toward the vast trunk in the distance.

Although the way was steep, Toots didn't find it tiring. She remembered how, when she'd been in the Upside-Down House with Olive, walking down stairs was always much more tiring than going up them. This, Olive had explained, was because when she was going up, she was really going down and vice versa. It had made Toots's brain buzz to try to figure that out, and now, as she climbed up the branch, she tried to puzzle it out again. With her mind busy on the problem, Toots was astonished to find that the next time she looked, the trunk was only a few feet away.

Craning back her neck, Toots stared up the tree. It looked as tall as a skyscraper! Toots expected that climbing it would be difficult and dangerous, but she was wrong. She soon saw that there were large crevices in the bark and she could actually climb inside these, which made it much safer. It was like climbing up an old, worn staircase with a banister of bark to keep her from falling. To stop herself from thinking about how long it would take her to reach the base of the tree, Toots concentrated on counting each step as she climbed.

She had just reached seven hundred when she

heard a noise that sounded like someone crying. It came from inside a knothole in the wood. Cautiously, Toots shone her flashlight through the hole. Behind the bark was a large cavern crammed full of tiny baby mites who were all sniffling and weeping quietly to themselves. Toots put her hand over the end of her flashlight to soften the light.

They must be Elizabeth's children! she thought. *Poor little things.*

The mite closest to her tried to raise its head, but it didn't have the strength. Toots knelt down beside it.

"What's the matter?" she whispered.

"We're hungry," it whimpered.

"So hungry," rasped another one.

"Please help us," begged a third.

"Don't worry," said Toots. "I'll get help."

A murmur ran through the cavern.

"Hurry, hurry. Please hurry!" the mites wailed.

"I will, I promise."

Toots squeezed back through the hole and continued her steady climb up the tree. Again she focused her mind and concentrated on each step, and almost before she knew it she had reached the bottom. She stood in the bark and, as she caught her breath, stared at the tangle of roots above her head.

A little way off, between two of the roots, there was a dark hole with a scar in the shape of the number three beside it. Toots smiled to herself. It was the entrance to landing bay number three. But the smile fell from her face as she realized that getting to the entrance was not going to be easy. It was only a few feet away, but the roots above her were smooth and bare without any foot- or hand-holds that she could see.

10 The Roots

It was horrible being able to see just where you wanted to go and not being able to get there. Toots was staring at the smooth roots when all at once she remembered what her father always told her to do whenever she was stuck with her homework. "Try and look at the problem from another angle" was his advice. "Look at it another way."

Toots twisted her head down and looked at the roots, but she still couldn't see any handholds, unless . . . She dipped her head a little farther over. Then she saw it. Just where the root ran along the ground it looked as though there was a ledge. Toots climbed up to the very top of the tree trunk and reached up with her hand to feel. It was a ledge all right, a little lip, and even though it was covered in the feathery white powder, it was just big enough for her hands to fit. She might be able to hang on to it and inch her way along to the hole. It wasn't going to be easy, but she didn't have a choice. Everything depended on her getting to that entrance. Everything. With both hands she grabbed hold of the ledge and swung out onto the root.

It was hard to hold on because the root bowed out toward her like a big belly, but Toots took a deep breath, slipped her right hand along the ledge, then slid her left up to meet it. In this way she advanced slowly, concentrating only on the movement of her hands.

Her fingers ached and she wished she could move faster, but she knew speeding up could be fatal. It was better to go slowly. She soldiered on until, at last, she was hanging right over the entrance. Now all she had to do was swing her legs just a little to the right and drop down. She didn't want to give herself time to get scared, so she counted to three, swung her legs over, and let go.

She landed just inside the tunnel and gasped with relief. She'd made it! But when she rolled over and looked deeper into the landing bay, her heart sank. The entrance was crammed tight with sharp furze-weed thorns. She stared back up at the root. There was no way now that she could reach it. She was trapped in the entrance.

"Ooooh," she said out loud, cross with herself for

getting in such a pickle. Suddenly, she felt cross about everything—about the way she'd got lost, about the way Olive hadn't been able to find her, about the way the wing commander had looked at her, and about the way Jemma had let her down. Toots gnawed her lip. Everything she thought about just made her more cross. And as she thought, the colors once again faded from the world, and her vision became tinged with gray.

Suddenly, the waspgnat's laugh shrieked all around her. Toots clamped her hands over her ears, but she couldn't blot out the awful sound. It was louder than she'd ever heard it before. She looked for some way to escape, but she was trapped. There was nowhere to run.

Then the furzeweed at the entrance of the landing bay untangled itself and a large gap appeared in the thorns. Through it, Toots could vaguely make out a row of landing lights in the distance.

She hesitated. Even though she wanted to get away from the waspgnat's wild laughter, she knew that if the thorns could move apart, they could just as easily move together again. What if she ran into the tunnel and the thorns squeezed her to death? The horrible laughter screamed even louder, and suddenly Toots didn't care what happened. She just had to escape from that noise!

The moment she ran through the hole in the

thorns, the waspgnat's laughter stopped. Toots was relieved and took her hands away from her ears, but an instant later there was a loud, whirring clatter as the thorns behind her snapped shut, sealing off her exit.

All the way along the tunnel, the thorns parted to let her pass, then closed behind her. Through the thick forest in front of her, Toots could still see the dim landing lights in the distance. Slowly she headed toward them, hoping that they would somehow show her the way out.

She stepped carefully onto what had once been the fairies' runway and set off following the line of lights, but when she got to where the doors should have been, there was no way through. Here the furzeweed did not stand aside. Instead, it crowded around the metal doors like iron filings around a magnet. Toots tried to pull the thorns away, but they wouldn't budge.

"Oh!" she cried, hitting the furzeweed angrily with her fists. Tears welled up in her eyes. The waspgnat's laughter rose again like a shrill wind, and this time a hundred raw voices joined with it and began to screech like birds.

Toots covered her ears. The waspgnat laughed louder. She pressed her hands harder against her ears, expecting the noise to go on forever, but just as suddenly as before, it stopped.

The silence was shocking. Toots gazed around her. The landing lights were growing dim. Or were they? No. They were just the same as they had been, but they were beginning to lose their color. It was as though someone had thrown a gray veil over them. Toots blinked. She'd felt like this before, when she'd been angry in the worm tunnels and at the entrance to the landing bay, but now the feeling was stronger, and the colors were fading fast. Within moments everything looked black and white and shades of gray, like an old film she'd once seen.

"What are you doing to my eyes?" she cried.

Her only answer came in a short burst of the bird-like chatter. A warm wind started to blow, and Toots grew frightened as the grayness in front of her began to break up into hazy shapes that danced through the air like wisps of gray silk. They were the same shapes she had seen in the tunnels. She could see their pale lemony eyes.

The bird-like chatter began again. It was louder this time. Toots wanted to cover her ears, but a thick band of gray smoke wrapped itself around her body, and she couldn't lift her hands away from her sides. She tried to cry out, but it was no use. A long, wispy strand covered her mouth, and a thick bandage of black smoke enveloped her eyes. As the twin lines of runway lights vanished, the waspgnat's laughter rose menacingly.

Smoky hands lifted Toots up. All around her the thorns clattered and the bird-like voices shrieked, and above it all the waspgnat laughed and laughed and laughed.

11 The Waspgnat's Lair

How far they carried her or for how long, Toots didn't know, but eventually she was set down, and the laughter and the bird-like screams and the clacking of the thorns stopped. The blackness in front of her eyes dissolved to gray, and Toots found to her relief that she could move freely.

She looked around and saw that she was in a huge domed chamber. The walls, the floor, and the ceiling were covered with tightly woven furzeweed. It was like being inside a basket. There were no doors or windows, but a thin yellow light shone between the interlaced thorns and threw crisscrossed shadows over the floor.

Cautiously, Toots moved around the edges of the chamber, trying to find a way out. She touched the wall, and the cavern shook with a thunderous din. The furzeweed contracted, and the light faded as the thorns drew closer together.

Toots leapt away and tripped as her foot caught between the thorns on the floor. Then something beneath the thorns grabbed hold of her foot. She tried to pull away, but whatever it was held on fast.

"Toots! Toots!" whispered a familiar voice. Toots stopped struggling and held still. "Toots, it's me, Olive!"

Toots peered down through the thorns of the floor and saw Olive's pale face staring up at her.

"Olive!" exclaimed Toots. "Are you all right?"

"The waspgnat knew why I had come," Olive whispered. Toots felt a twinge of guilt. "It's been trying to make me into a wraith." Olive smiled weakly. "But it hasn't managed it yet. I guess I'm a tough nut to crack."

"Olive, don't worry, I'll get you out of here."

"Be careful, Toots," whispered Olive. "And keep moving. The wraiths can only get a good hold of you if you stand still."

Toots stood up and looked around. "There has to be a way out of here," she whispered to herself.

All at once the yellow light grew brighter.

"Oh, but there is, my dear," murmured a laughing voice. And though the voice was as sweet as Christmas bells, Toots felt her heart grow cold.

"Indeed there is," the waspgnat continued. "And such an easy way, such a very easy way." Toots spun around but could see no one.

"Toots!" said Olive "Don't forget, guard your mind. Remember, it can read your thoughts."

The waspgnat laughed again, and the thorns rippled all around the walls like waves on the ocean.

"Ah, Toots. At last. We're so glad to meet you," said the waspgnat with a soft laugh. "We were beginning to think you would never get here."

"What do you want?" Toots cried.

Her voice echoed around the cavern and bounced back ten times louder than before. *What do you want?*

"Stop it!" she shouted. But the echo shouted back at her, *"Stop it . . . Stop it . . . Stop it . . . ,"* and the laughter shrieked above it.

"Oh, dear. Poor, poor Toots," the waspgnat whispered in a singsongy way. "Let's get a better look at you."

Above her, the thorns in the ceiling clacked angrily. Toots looked up. They were unlacing at the top of the dome and settling in a thick bank around the edges of the cavern. The yellow light was growing stronger. As her eyes grew accustomed to it, she began to see that something gnarled and ancient was sprawled across the ceiling. Toots shuddered.

It was the waspgnat.

It looked like an old, mangled root vegetable that had been left to rot. Its body was a bulbous mound surrounded by a jumble of limbs. They crossed and crisscrossed each other like so many moldy parsnips with long, stringy ends. A thin wisp of black smoke curled from the tip of each limb and coiled into the air, fading among the gray shapes.

For a moment Toots felt relieved. The horrible gray shapes were nothing but a little smoke.

The soft voice laughed again. "Oh, no, not just smoke, my dear. Oh, no, no, no, not just smoke. These are my little friends, my children, my workers. These are my wraiths, and they've been so looking forward to meeting you."

The waspgnat lifted its limbs, releasing puffs of smoke that shot out and swirled through the air. Toots could see faces with narrow yellow eyes and sharp, mean little mouths in the smoke. The wraiths opened their mouths and chattered like birds at dawn.

Toots watched, mesmerized, as they danced through the air. They twirled and somersaulted and flew right up to the ceiling, twisting in and out of the tangled thorns.

"Wouldn't you like to play with my pretties?" asked the waspgnat in its soft voice. "Doesn't it look like fun?"

One shadowy creature brushed against her. It was warm and soft and it tickled her. Despite herself Toots laughed.

"Would you like to fly?" cooed the waspgnat. "Would that be nice? Why don't you give it a go?"

Two thin shadows wrapped themselves around Toots's arms. Yellow eyes gazed up at her. Mean little mouths smiled. Toots felt a slight pressure on her arms; then suddenly she was lifted off the ground.

Toots laughed again. She couldn't help it. The wraiths on either side of her swooped like swallows, guiding her over the bank of thorns and up toward the waspgnat, where it smoldered on the ceiling.

"That's right, my pretties," cooed the waspgnat. "Bring her close to me. Bring her up and let me have a nice, long look at her."

Suddenly, flying was no fun at all. Toots didn't want to get close to that strange, foul-smelling root. She tried to pull away from the wraiths, but the smoky shapes were deceptively strong. The wraiths' eyes mocked her as she struggled.

"Oh, dear," laughed the soft voice. "You wanted to come up here, but now you want to run away. This will never do."

As it said this, part of the bulbous mound rolled back. Two thin yellow eyes with jet-black pupils stared at her, and a grinning slit of a mouth like a knife wound opened in the pulpy ocher flesh.

It was the face Toots had seen so many times hiding in the thorns, only now it was much bigger and much more terrifying.

The mouth opened wider, baring two rows of tiny yellow teeth. Wisps of gray smoke curled in and out of the mouth and looped around a charcoal-black tongue.

"What's the matter, my dear?" asked the soft voice. "You seem taken aback. Surely you're not afraid of me? After all, we know each other so well."

Toots's eyes widened in horror. What did it mean by that?

The waspgnat laughed, and as it shifted, the fat folds of its flesh revealed a large purple rock embedded in its chest.

The olm! she thought, but as soon as she thought it, she regretted it.

"Do you think I don't know why you're here?" it snickered. "Just like that other one, you came here to steal my jewel, my power, my precious olm."

The waspgnat laughed again, and Toots almost choked on the clouds of billowing smoke. Around the chamber the wraiths laughed, too, high and shrill like a hundred hungry starlings.

Toots coughed and spluttered, and her eyes smarted from the smoke. She had to get away from this vile and poisonous thing, but she couldn't move against the wraiths' firm grasp.

"You can't leave so soon." The waspgnat's voice broke a little now. Roughened by the smoke, it had lost its softness and had taken on a menacing edge. "I'd like to keep you with me, always. You belong here with my little family."

"No!" cried Toots, trying to turn her head away. But wisps of smoke poured out of the waspgnat's eyes and formed themselves into claw-like hands. They held her head so she could not look away.

Toots found herself staring deep into those terrible eyes. All colors faded to gray, and sudden angry thoughts crowded into her brain. She was furious with Olive for letting her get lost and for bringing her to the Upside-Down World in the first place. She was scalding mad at Jemma, ten times as cross as she had been on the day of the car wash.

"Good, good," the waspgnat murmured, licking its lips.

Cross thoughts crowded into Toots's head without rhyme or reason. Little hurts became huge annoyances. She was angry with Binky for digging his dog holes. She was livid about the wing commander's being so rude to her.

The waspgnat rolled its eyes back in its head and laughed so hard that the smoke clouded the air.

Toots felt shaken and faint and very close to tears. The waspgnat had changed. It had grown larger and stronger. The folds of flesh around the olm were pushed back, and the olm itself was brighter and bigger.

The waspgnat smiled, and its nasty mouth seemed big enough to swallow her in one gulp. For a moment Toots thought that this was what it was going to do, but the waspgnat only laughed.

"Oh, dear me, no, child, I don't want to eat you. You are far too valuable as you are. Where would I be without you?"

Toots was falling into the waspgnat's fathomless eyes again when suddenly an earsplitting howl tore through the chamber.

"*Whaaooooo-wooo-wooo-wooo!*"

Toots looked down into the cavern and saw Binky. He threw back his head and wailed.

"*Whaaoooo! Whaoooooo!*"

"Binky!" she said. Behind Binky she could see the hole he had dug through the furzeweed. At his feet there was another hole, and Olive was already climbing through it.

"Arghh!" screamed the waspgnat. "Look what it's done to my beautiful furzeweed! Get that animal. Get it!"

All the wraiths, save for the two that held Toots tight, raced down toward Binky and Olive. Binky howled again, and Olive quickly unlooped her coil of cobweb rope and twirled it above her head like a lasso.

Wraiths circled Olive, trying to get a hold on her, but she wafted them away with the lasso, dancing a mad sort of hula. Binky ran around in circles and wriggled furiously so that the wraiths couldn't get hold of him.

"Don't worry, Toots. I'll get you down!" Olive cried.

"Look at me, Toots," insisted the waspgnat. "Look at me."

Against her will, Toots turned back to face the creature on the ceiling. The yellow eyes were now as bright as flames.

"You're not going anywhere," hissed the wasp-gnat. "You belong here with me."

Toots tried to say no, tried to shout, to scream, but she couldn't make any noise. She could only stare into those terrifying yellow eyes and nod.

Then Olive's lasso looped over her foot, and she felt a tug at her ankle. Toots dropped several feet toward the floor. The wraiths holding her scowled and pulled at her arms, but Olive and her cobweb rope were stronger. Olive tugged again, and Toots dropped all the way to the floor.

Binky snapped at the wraiths holding her arms, biting them into nothing but wispy scraps of smoke.

"Are you all right?" Olive asked urgently.

"I don't know," replied Toots. She felt shaky and strange. "I—"

"I'll take a proper look at you after we get out of here," said Olive. "The furzeweed will find a way to close that hole soon enough. Let's go!"

Olive hurried Toots toward Binky's hole. All around them the furzeweed shuddered and clacked, trying to bring its sharp thorns across the hole. But for the moment, it couldn't seal the gap. Binky shot through, and Toots was about to follow, when the waspgnat suddenly screamed, *"Away, wraiths! Let me have them!"*

In an instant the smoky wraiths vanished.

Toots looked up at the ceiling and froze.

"Go!" cried Olive, but Toots couldn't move. She was fascinated and terrified at the same time.

"It's coming down," she whispered.

The waspgnat plucked its rootish limbs out of the ceiling and started down the wall, scuttling like a spider, hunchbacked and foul. Then it stopped and raised itself up so that Toots could see the purple rock, the olm, embedded in its chest.

"Olive, the olm!" cried Toots. If only she could smash that rock! If only she could destroy the olm, then everything would be all right.

"I can hear your thoughts, Toots," the waspgnat purred. "I know what you want. Why don't you come and get it?"

"Toots, no!" Olive insisted. "Now isn't the time. It will destroy you."

But Toots didn't hear. Quickly she hunted in Olive's bucket and pulled out a hammer. That would do the trick. Toots turned and brandished the hammer.

"Come on," the waspgnat whispered, taunting

her. "Here it is. Look how strong it is. How do you think it got that way? I didn't come to the garden uninvited, you know. Who do you think brought me to the garden? Who do you think?"

Olive grabbed Toots and dragged her back to the hole in the furzeweed.

"Toots, you wouldn't stand a chance," Olive puffed as she half carried Toots away.

"I have to try!" cried Toots.

"That's what it wants you to do, can't you see?" cried Olive.

"Most of this garden is mine already," the wasp-gnat shouted after them. "Now I'm going to get the rest!"

Olive pushed Toots down the hole after Binky, leaving the shrieking wraiths and the clacking thorns behind.

12 Back to Headquarters

When Toots emerged at the other end of the hole, Binky was waiting for her. He barked joyfully and leapt up at her, licking her face and ears. Toots didn't have the strength to push him away.

"That wasn't an idle threat the waspgnat made," warned Olive as she wriggled out of the hole. "It certainly looks strong enough to take over the garden. Let's get back to headquarters. The evacuation should be well under way by now." They quickly blocked up the hole with soil. "It's not much," said Olive, patting down the dirt. "But it might keep the furzeweed at bay for a little while."

Olive took Toots's flashlight and switched it on. They were back in the worm tunnels. The dark walls sparkled. Olive felt along the right-hand side of the wall. "Oh, thank goodness," she said, finding her finger marks. Toots took the light and shone it on the opposite wall. There were finger marks there, too.

"Oh, no," said Olive. "Which way should we go?"

Luckily Binky knew. He sniffed the ground, then set off, barking for the others to follow.

"Well done!" said Olive as she and Toots hurried to keep up with the eager little dog.

They soon reached the dog holes. Olive flew first Binky and then Toots across the first one they came to. At the next, where there wasn't enough room to fly, she used the cobweb rope and the grappling hooks and swung them over one at a time. Now all they had to do was follow the trail of blue wool. But there was no time to lose, for already there were large dark stains growing on the walls.

"The furzeweed is following us," gasped Olive. "There's no time to waste."

The stain on one wall began to buckle, and suddenly a huge furzeweed thorn shot out into the tunnel. Toots yelped and set off at a run after Olive and Binky.

Far behind them they could hear the screams of the wraiths and the clack-clack of the furzeweed's thorns. Toots tried not to listen. On and on they ran, never pausing to catch their breath.

As Toots ran in the darkness, her thoughts ran on in her head. What had the waspgnat meant when it said it didn't come to the garden uninvited?

Who or what would invite a waspgnat into a garden? thought Toots. *And how?* Then she remembered the angry thoughts that had rushed through her head when the waspgnat had had her in its grip. She thought of how much stronger it had looked when it let her go. *Does the waspgnat feed on bad feelings?* she wondered. *Does it grow on angry thoughts?*

If that were true, then maybe someone *could* attract a waspgnat.

Toots was so lost in thought she only noticed that Olive had stopped when she ran right into her.

"Wait," said Olive, switching off the flashlight.

A little way ahead, the tunnel glowed with an eerie white light. Above the noise of the wraiths and the furzeweed, they could hear something wailing.

"What is it?" whispered Toots.

"I'm not sure," replied Olive.

They crept forward. The light grew brighter and the wailing more distinct. Binky crept stealthily ahead of them. With his head low and his ears flat, he vanished around the next corner.

Moments later they heard him howl so piteously that Toots cried out, "Binky!" and hurried after him.

She didn't have to go far. Around the next corner she found the maggot sisters, Blanche and Palydia, slowly making their way up the tunnel. They were in a terrible state. Their skin was flaking off, their fine clothes were in tatters, they had lost their feather crowns and their spectacles, and their eyes were red and raw from crying. Blanche was struggling with a bulging suitcase, while Palydia carried the heavy mincing machine in a basket. All their furniture and worldly goods moved slowly in a towering stack behind them.

"Why do we have to leave our lovely home?" whined Blanche through her almost dried-up lips.

"Can't we just stay?" sobbed Palydia, crying even louder.

Toots, Olive, and Binky hurried up to them.

"Oh!" wailed the sisters, shying away from Binky's snuffling nose. "Don't hurt us!"

"Where's Elizabeth?" asked Toots. "What have you done with her?"

"That dreadful stuff invaded our home," Palydia sniffed.

"Nasty sharp thorns," cried Blanche.

"Our lovely home, all gone, all gone!" wailed Palydia.

"Toots, we've got to hurry," urged Olive. Binky barked. The screeching wraiths were getting closer, and more dark stains were growing on the walls.

"What have you done with Elizabeth?" Toots demanded again. Blanche pointed a tattered finger at the huge stack of furniture. It took Toots a moment to realize that Elizabeth's small brown face was poking out from beneath all the chairs and tables and mirrors and folded curtains. The poor little mite was carrying the whole lot on her back!

"Oh, Elizabeth," gasped Toots, pushing past the maggots. "How cruel!"

"Don't blame us. She insisted on carrying it all," explained Palydia, dropping her basket.

"Yes, it was all her idea," insisted Blanche, sitting down, *flump*, on her suitcase.

Toots ignored them. Taking the mite's knife, she cut through the ropes that tied the furniture to Elizabeth's back. With a heave Toots pushed the chairs and tables and curtains to the floor. The mirrors smashed against the wall. "Olive, shine the light over here," said Toots.

"Now hold still, Elizabeth," she said, studying the tangle of wire around the mite's muzzle. Toots blew on her fingers, then, ignoring the ever louder wails of the waspgnat's wraiths and the clacking of the thorns, she gently and speedily set to work.

"Oh, thank you," gasped Elizabeth as Toots unfastened the last knot in the wire. Elizabeth opened her mouth wide with relief.

"Toots," insisted Olive. "We've got to go." Olive was right. The furzeweed was not far behind them now, and the warm wind of the wraiths had begun to blow through the tunnel.

"Oh!" wailed Blanche and Palydia.

Elizabeth rushed back to them. "They'll be in terrible danger if we leave them," she said, helping Blanche to her feet.

"Elizabeth's right," said Olive. "We have to take them with us. But they can't bring their baggage. We'll move much faster without it."

Olive put an arm around Blanche and half carried her, and Elizabeth and Toots supported the wailing Palydia, while Binky ran ahead to lead the way through the dark tunnel.

With Binky's smart nose and the blue wool to guide them, they soon came to the end of the worm tunnels and found themselves back in the deserted corridors of fairy headquarters. Their quick footsteps rang out along the prettily tiled floor.

The corridor had been abandoned in a hurry. Doors were half open, lights were left on, and half-packed baskets lay haphazardly in the corridor. Olive pushed them out of the way as they hurried past.

They hadn't gone very far along the corridor when there was a great clatter of thorns behind them. Toots looked back. The entrance to the worm tunnels was now completely blocked with thorns, and more were sprouting by the second. Cracks raced along the green painted walls, splitting the plaster as the thorns fought their way through.

"Come on," commanded Olive. "If anyone's left, they'll be in the emergency landing bay. Quickly, this way."

Toots and Elizabeth ran faster, half pulling, half carrying Palydia between them.

Olive turned down a corridor on the left. At the far end of it, Toots could see large metal doors and a sign that said LANDING BAY NUMBER ONE. EMERGENCY EVACUATIONS ONLY. They raced toward it.

With terrifying speed, the furzeweed broke through the walls and the ceiling. Toots could hear the horrible chatter of the wraiths, and somewhere far behind that the shrieking laughter of the waspgnat. She tried to block it out of her mind.

When they reached the landing bay doors, Olive gently set the exhausted Blanche on the ground and tried to open the doors. But they were shut fast.

Olive set her ear against the doors and listened. "I can hear something. I think there's someone still in there."

The doors to the landing bay were at a T-junction in the corridor. Blanche looked to the left and Palydia to the right, and both of them screamed as, with a loud and hideous clatter, the furzeweed broke through both sides simultaneously. Now the attack would come from all *three* directions at once. Their only hope was to get into the landing bay and find a way out from there.

The warm wind gathered strength, and the corridor grew dark with thorns. Olive hammered on the door. "Hello, is anyone there? It's Olive Brown. . . .

Can you hear me? Please let us in. This is an emergency!"

Toots looked behind and her heart leapt into her throat as the long, wrinkled limbs and hideous head of the waspgnat appeared at the far end of the corridor. It opened its horrible mouth and laughed. Smoke flooded out from between its teeth. Toots shut her eyes.

Olive banged on the door again. "Hello? Please let us in!" she yelled.

The thorns were less than fifteen feet away now and closing in quickly. The ceiling cracked and thorns shot down. The floor buckled and thorns shot up.

"Brown? Brown, is that you?" bellowed a voice through the door.

"Wing Commander?" gasped Olive. "Yes, ma'am. Please hurry, let us in!"

Then, above the noise of the furzeweed and the wraiths, Toots heard bolts shooting back and bars being lifted from the other side of the door. Suddenly, the doors opened just wide enough for them to slip through.

Olive made sure that Blanche, Palydia, Binky, Elizabeth, and Toots were safely through, then quickly went in herself. Once inside, they all leaned against the doors to close them before the furzeweed or the wraiths could force their way in. The waspgnat scuttled forward, and just as the door closed, the tiniest wisp of its smoke blew into Toots's face. The waspgnat's voice echoed in her head.

"Who do you think brought me to the garden? Who do you think?"

13 | Landing Bay Number One

There was quite a crowd in the landing bay. Every fairy from the Upside-Down Garden was there, and even though they all looked exhausted, several of them rushed to help Olive and Elizabeth carry the sisters into a quiet corner. Blanche and Palydia complained bitterly.

"No . . . no. We don't want to sit down. We're not tired," they wailed. But the instant they sat down, they fell fast asleep.

The rest of the fairies were working hard, covering the walls, the floor, and the ceiling with metal from flattened baked-bean cans, hammering each tin piece in place. Others chipped at a great rock in the corner. Wing Commander Lewis walked back to a table in the middle of the room, where the group captain was studying a map.

Toots watched the wing commander closely.

"Who do you think brought me to the garden?"

the waspgnat had asked. *Could it have been the wing commander?* Toots wondered.

Outside in the corridor, the wraiths screeched. The furzeweed pounded against the doors and against the tin-covered floor, ceiling, and walls. It threatened to break through at any moment.

The wing commander stood by the table, talking earnestly with the group captain. Then the group captain summoned Olive to the table. Olive stood in front of her with her head bowed. Toots couldn't hear what the group captain was saying, but she could guess what was happening. Olive was being reprimanded for disobeying orders and seeking out the waspgnat. And all the time the wing commander stood behind the group captain, saying nothing in Olive's defense. Nobody noticed as Toots crept closer to the table.

"This is very serious," the group captain was saying. "I'm afraid, Olive, that you're going to have to take full responsibility."

"Yes, ma'am, I know. I'm sorry," answered Olive, hanging her head.

This was more than Toots could stand.

"Stop!" she screamed, rushing to the table. "It was nothing to do with Olive. It was all the wing commander's fault! *She* did it! *She's* the one who brought the waspgnat to the garden!"

The landing bay became very still. Toots looked

around. Olive, the group captain, the wing commander, and all the fairies were staring at her. Beyond the doors, the furzeweed had stopped pounding and the wraiths had ceased their screeching. The only sound was the laughter of the wasp-gnat.

"It's all the wing commander's fault," Toots said again, but this time she didn't sound quite so sure of herself.

Toots didn't understand. Everything had seemed so clear a moment before! But now her thoughts were fuzzy and muddled. One hot tear slid down her cheek. She felt so foolish.

Outside, the furzeweed began to pound again and the wraiths to screech anew.

"Oh!" cried Toots, clamping her hands over her ears.

"Everyone back to work!" cried the wing commander, shooing the other fairies away. "We must make sure the furzeweed can't break in here. Keep hammering the tin in place."

Olive gently wrapped an arm about Toots's shoulders and guided her to a chair.

"I've made such a mess of things," sobbed Toots, burying her face in her hands.

"It's all right," replied Olive. "You just got hold of the wrong end of the stick, that's all."

"But I thought . . . ," began Toots. "I thought it

was the wing commander's hate and anger that brought the waspgnat to the garden."

"Oh, no," said Olive softly. "The wing commander would never do anything to harm the garden. When she was in charge of one down by the river, that garden's human fell out with his son, and a wasp—" Olive stopped herself. "Well, come on, we've got plenty to do."

Toots slowly lifted her head. "You mean . . . you mean . . . *humans* bring waspgnats to the garden?" she asked.

Olive was quiet for moment. "Yes," she said.

Toots closed her eyes and groaned. Everything seemed to come together at once. She remembered how the wing commander had said, "The tree's not the problem!" She remembered the way the waspgnat had said, "Where would I be without you?" But clearest of all, she remembered the day she'd first heard the waspgnat's laughter in the wind. It was the day she had fallen out with Jemma.

Once more the waspgnat's question roared through her head. "Who do you think brought me to the garden?"

"I did," Toots said. "I brought the waspgnat here, didn't I?" She opened her eyes and looked around. All of the fairies were staring at her. Toots could see by their sympathetic looks that they all knew, that they'd always known. She felt wretched.

"Why didn't you tell me?" she whispered.

"We couldn't," said the group captain softly. "You had to find out for yourself. You were always the only one who could destroy the waspgnat. That's why Olive brought you down here. But perhaps the wing commander was right all along. It was too great a risk."

Toots looked over at the wing commander. Now she knew why the wing commander didn't like humans, and she couldn't blame her. This would be the second garden she'd lost because of them, and Toots wished with all her heart that it wasn't so.

Beyond the doors the wraiths squawked like demented crows. The furzeweed banged so violently that the walls were beginning to buckle under the pressure.

"Come on, Toots," said Olive as she gently took hold of Toots's wrist and tried to pull her to her feet. "We have to find a way out of here, and we need you to help us. You have to look at these maps."

"Olive, I can't," replied Toots. She just wanted to sit there and feel bad.

"You must," insisted Olive, forcing Toots to her feet.

It was only then that Toots noticed there was something very wrong in the landing bay. With the furzeweed hammering at the doors, the fairies should have been evacuating as fast as they could.

And yet not one of them was leaving. In the far corner a group of fairies were digging holes in the floor between the panels of tin, while others were chipping away at a mound of rock. Toots stared at the rock. It covered almost the whole wall at the end of the runway and was completely blocking the fairies' exit.

"There's the problem, you see," said the wing commander. "That rock is fairly new. It wasn't there the last time we checked this landing bay." She pointed to the map on the table. "Our maps must be woefully out-of-date. We're trying to dig our way out through the ground, but we keep hitting stone."

"If we don't find a way out soon, it will be too late," the group captain said, swallowing hard.

"Don't worry," said the wing commander. "Toots will think of something. I'm sure of it."

This took Toots by surprise. She glanced up and was amazed to see the wing commander wink at her.

Toots turned back to the table and stared at the map of the garden. It was highly detailed. It showed all the tunnels beneath the ground and the locations of the landing bays, all but one of which had been crossed off with a large red X. Lying on top of this was a sheet of tracing paper that showed a plan of the garden as the humans knew it. This way, the map showed both the Right-Side-Up Garden and the Upside-Down Garden at the same time.

Toots stared at it. There was the tree and the path and the fishpond and the beginning of the house, and there was the lawn and the flower beds, but something was missing. She shook her head. What was it? The garden in the drawing looked somehow out-of-date.

That was it! This map had been made *before* her father built the patio by the house, before he put down the crazy paving!

Toots grabbed the wing commander's pencil. "Look," she said excitedly. "My father has just covered all of this area with paving stones. They're not regular, they're strange shapes. We call it crazy paving."

"Crazy paving?" whispered Olive, the group captain, and the wing commander together.

"Yes," replied Toots as she quickly drew the crazy paving in on the map. "It reaches from the house to about here. That's why you can't dig through the ground."

"Stop digging!" bellowed the wing commander. All the fairies stopped. "So how can we get through this?"

Toots ran over to the mound of rock at the end of the runway. "Is this where the exit used to be?" she asked.

The wing commander and the group captain nodded.

"This isn't a rock," Toots said, pressing her hands against the rough surface. "It's cement. My father must have blocked up the hole before he laid the paving stones."

Toots stared at the cement. There was so much of it. At the rate they'd been going, it would take the fairies from now until forever to chip through it all. They would have to find another way out of the landing bay. Toots narrowed her eyes, then nodded.

"Binky!" she cried. "Come here, boy." Binky ran to her side. Toots picked up a small piece of cement and held it out. Binky sniffed it thoroughly.

"Go seek," whispered Toots. "Go seek over there." She pointed to the middle of the floor where the fairies had been digging. With one quick yap, Binky scampered over and set his nose to the ground.

Suddenly, his tail wagged, and he began to scratch at the tin on the ground. "There it is!" cried Toots. "Pull off the tin and dig where Binky is scratching. You'll find a crack between the paving stones. There'll be less cement there, and it will be easier to break through."

"Everybody dig where the dog says!" cried the wing commander. "Good work, Toots," she said out of the side of her mouth. Olive nudged Toots with her elbow.

The fairies quickly pulled up the sheet of metal, then got to work with their picks and hammers, chipping away along the line that Binky had indicated. Within minutes one fairy had chipped a tiny hole right through the cement and could see daylight beyond it. The fairies now worked together to make the hole bigger. It was only a matter of moments before it was large enough for a single fairy to squeeze through without crumpling her wings.

"Will everyone be able to get out of that hole?" asked Toots, looking at the large wing commander doubtfully.

"Ssshhh," whispered the wing commander. "We don't want the waspgnat to know our plans. Don't forget it can hear everything, even our thoughts."

Just then there was a scream from the fairies who were guarding the doors. One long sharp thorn of furzeweed had managed to squeeze between the crack in the doors and was now forcing them open.

Toots, Olive, Elizabeth, and the wing commander hurried over.

"If only I felt hungry," gasped Elizabeth as she pressed hard against the door. "Furzeweed used to be my favorite food. I'd have been able to chomp through a thorn like this in no time at all."

Everyone looked at her in surprise.

"That's why the maggots muzzled me," she explained. "They didn't want me to eat their beauty cream. Hah! They didn't know I wasn't hungry. I haven't been hungry since I lost my little ones. I haven't been hungry at all."

Toots's eyes lit up. "You mean," she whispered, "you mean you would eat this if you knew where your children were?"

"Faster than a fairy can fly."

Olive spoke up. "Careful, Toots," she urged. "Remember that the waspgnat is close enough to be able to read your thoughts."

Toots nodded. "What about your children?" she asked Elizabeth. "Do they like furzeweed, too?"

"Oh, yes, they have fine appetites," Elizabeth said.

"I . . . I . . . I . . ." Toots could hardly speak because she was so excited. "Olive, Elizabeth, I know where they are."

Elizabeth's face lit up. "You do?"

"They're hidden in a knot halfway up the tree. I saw them there this morning."

"Oh, my babies! Were they all right?"

"They said they were hungry. Very hungry." Toots's eyes twinkled.

The wing commander beamed at her. "Can you hold the door without me? I must tell the group captain," she said.

Elizabeth nodded. "I'll do better than that," and she reached up and took a huge bite out of the thorn and then another and another until it was almost gone. Another thorn shot through, and Elizabeth bit into this one, too.

The wing commander hurried to the group captain. Within moments the wing commander barked, "I want twenty flyers to go on the double to the knot halfway up the tree, recover hidden treasure, and bring it back here immediately. None of you is to think about this mission. Remember that all your thoughts can be read."

The flyers slipped one by one through the hole in the floor and out into the garden.

Although Elizabeth quickly ate every thorn that squeezed through the doors, she was starting to get full. The furzeweed was forcing the doors farther open, and everyone had to double their efforts to keep them closed.

"I wish they'd hurry back," said Toots.

"Stop thinking about it," warned Olive.

Toots nodded and tried to think of nothing. But her mind was racing. It was full of thoughts.

"I can't think of nothing," she said. "I keep thinking of things."

"I know it's hard," puffed Olive. "But if you can't think of nothing, think of something in the past that isn't important. Or say one phrase over and over again. That should still your thoughts."

So Toots tried to think of what she could say over

and over again that would make her thoughts stay still. She tried a tongue twister, *She sells seashells on the seashore*, but it was too hard and she soon gave up. She tried just to say *butter* over and over again, but her mind soon wandered. Then suddenly she hit upon something that Olive had said earlier. And as she repeated it, she felt her mind hold absolutely still. She had never felt so clearheaded before.

We've got to get to the root of the problem. The root of the problem. The root of the problem, she said.

The furzeweed pushed the doors open just a little wider and more thorns shot through. Elizabeth could only eat so much. Everyone pushed against the thorns, but they couldn't shut the doors.

Beyond the tangle Toots could see the waspgnat with its horrible limbs crushed into what had been the fairies' corridor. Its face bulged as it opened its mouth wide to laugh, and there embedded in its chest was the olm. Toots wished with all her heart that she could have broken that stone and robbed the waspgnat of its power. But as she thought this, the waspgnat laughed louder.

The root of the problem, the root of the problem, the root of the problem! Toots shouted in her mind. Then suddenly she had an idea. It came to her in a flash and was so dangerous and so wonderful that she quickly hid it deep in her mind.

Instead, she concentrated on pushing the doors

shut. With one almighty shove, Olive and Toots and
Elizabeth managed to close the doors enough so that
the wing commander could fix a wooden bar across
them. That would hold them for a little while. Toots
knew that she had very little time. She had to act fast.

"Olive, I have to go," she said. "And I need to
take Binky with me."

"What? Right now?" Olive asked. Then she
looked hard at Toots. "You have a plan, don't you?"

Toots nodded. "I can't explain," she said.

"No, you mustn't," warned Olive. "Don't even
try."

The wing commander stepped forward. "I'll send
her back," she boomed. "Come on, then." She took
Toots by the shoulder and led her to the hole.

Toots scooped Binky up in her arms and looked
back at Olive one last time. Olive nodded her
encouragement and smiled.

The wing commander knelt down beside Toots
and fastened one end of a cobweb rope to Toots's
wrist. She pulled out a clean white handkerchief and
handed it to Toots. "Make sure you're always touching this so you don't forget us," she said. Toots
nodded and, remembering how she'd forgotten
everything when she'd put the bucket in her pocket,
she tucked the handkerchief down inside her sock,
making sure it was next to her skin.

Then the wing commander leaned forward and

said in a quiet voice that only Toots could hear, "Good luck, Toots, with whatever it is you're planning." The wing commander looked Toots in the eye and smiled. "I think I'm learning new things about humans today. You've been so very brave already. We're a rare breed, you and me and Olive. There're not many who have faced a waspgnat and survived to tell the tale."

Toots's eyes grew wide. "Then it was you," she gasped "*You* were the fairy who knew about the olm. *You* were the one who tried to save the other garden."

"Shush," said the wing commander as she finished tying the rope. "Let's keep that our secret." Toots suddenly saw the wing commander in a new light and would have said something, but the wing commander stood up briskly.

"Get a move on, then," she said in her normal rough voice. But Toots had to say one last thing. She leaned forward and whispered urgently, "Please, you must make sure that everyone keeps over to the far side of the landing bay. I don't want anyone to get—"

"Shush." The wing commander put a warning finger to her lips and nodded. "I'll make sure it's done. Hurry now. Good-bye, Toots, and be brave."

"I'll try, I promise," replied Toots.

Toots nodded at the wing commander, then slipped through the hole, clutching Binky in her arms. As she dangled with her feet pointing down toward the endless sky, she craned her neck and looked up at the crazy paving above her. She watched the huge, field-sized yellow and gray stones grow smaller. Far away in the shadow of the tree, the squadron of fairies were setting off with their arms full of hungry baby mites.

Toots tried to keep her mind blank. *The root of the problem, the root of the problem.*

She was so busy trying to think of nothing that she didn't realize she was back to her normal size until she hit the ground. The paving stones were cold and hard beneath her knees. Binky landed beside her, jumped to his feet, and began hurriedly to sniff the ground. Toots felt the cobweb rope yank against her wrist, then slip away. The wing commander must have taken it back, she thought. Toots stared down at the little hole in the cement between the paving stones. It was a tiny crack, no bigger than an ant hole.

"I won't let you down, Olive," she whispered. "I won't let you down."

14 Back in the Garden

Toots knelt on the ground and ran her hand over the smooth paving stone. If her guess was correct, the waspgnat was under the crazy-paving stone to the right of the hole. From the way Binky was snuffling over that spot, she knew she was right. She put her ear to the ground and listened for the waspgnat's evil laugh, then picked up a pebble and used it to scratch a big X across the paving stone.

Toots leapt up and raced to her father's tool shed. Binky ran after her, barking at her heels. She flung open the door and grabbed a chisel, a screwdriver, and a hammer. She was about to run back when she noticed a long-handled sledgehammer leaning by the door.

That will do the trick, she thought. *If I can lift it.*

Toots put down the other tools and picked up the

sledgehammer. It was heavy, but with an effort she dragged it out onto the crazy paving.

Toots clapped her hands next to the hole in the paving stone.

"Everybody out of the way!" she warned any invisible fairies. "Stand back!"

She picked up the sledgehammer with both hands, then swung it above her head and let it drop on the X with an almighty crash. A crack ran across the paving stone from one side to the other and thin wisps of black and gray smoke trickled out. But the stone was not broken.

Toots lifted the hammer again and brought it down with all her might. The paving stone shattered. Clouds of black smoke billowed out around the head of the hammer and dispersed in the wind.

"Toots, what on earth do you think you are doing?" cried her father as he rushed around the side of the house. She had forgotten that he had arranged to be home early. She had forgotten that he was going to help Mr. Phelps cut down the tree.

"My patio!" he cried as he pulled the sledge-hammer out of her hands. "You've ruined it. What on earth possessed you to do such a thing?"

"Afternoon, Mr. Wheate," said Mr. Phelps, tipping back his hat as he came into the garden. He nodded when he saw the ruined paving stone and the sledgehammer in Toots's father's hands. "Getting rid of the paving, are you? Can't say I blame you. I like a nice big lawn myself. Much better." Mr. Phelps winked at Toots.

"No, I'm not getting rid of it," said her father in his most exasperated voice.

Mr. Phelps nodded down at Binky, who was digging furiously at the smashed stone. "Looks like that young fellow wants to get rid of it, at any rate," he said.

"Oh!" cried Toots's father. He grabbed Binky by the collar and pulled him away.

Toots gasped. Between the fragments of the smashed stone she could see the waspgnat. The foul thing was old and yellow, and in the sunlight its limbs glistened with slime. It was disgusting, and Toots, her father, and Mr. Phelps shied away from its sulfurous smoke with their hands over their noses. The waspgnat wriggled and writhed furiously. It seemed to be trying to burrow back into the earth. Suddenly, Binky broke free from Toots's father and lunged toward it. With a snap of his jaws, he bit deep into one of the waspgnat's limbs and began to pull.

Toots latched onto Binky's collar and tried to help him pull it out, but the waspgnat was too strong.

"Dad, help," she panted.

Her father regained his grip on Binky's collar, but though he and Toots pulled together, they couldn't shift the waspgnat.

"All right now, let's work this as a team," said Mr. Phelps. He jammed a broad spade in the broken stones. "When I count to three, you all pull as hard as you can, and I'll see if we can shift it. One . . . two . . . three!"

With all of them pulling and Mr. Phelps levering the spade, the waspgnat shot out of the hole. Binky, Toots, and her father fell backward onto the lawn.

The waspgnat lay smoldering on the grass. Its horrible laugh was now a thin squeal. It sounded like air escaping from a punctured balloon.

"Would you look at that?" said Mr. Phelps, taking off his hat and wafting away the smoke. The waspgnat writhed in the sunlight, desperately trying to find a way to get back underground.

"What is it?" asked Toots's father.

Binky yelped and ran to his water bowl. He drank noisily, desperate to wash the vile taste from his mouth.

"Well, I'll be jiggered. It could be the answer to your prayers," said Mr. Phelps mysteriously. "We'll have to wait and see." He looked up at the tree thoughtfully.

Toots crouched down to look at the waspgnat. Even though she was so much bigger now, it still sent shivers of fear running up and down her spine. She could see the waspgnat's thin yellow eyes and the slit of its ugly, smoking mouth. And its high-pitched squeal was so evil it terrified her even more than its laugh.

Toots's father picked up a long stick and flipped the waspgnat onto its back. The piercing squeal grew louder.

Toots gasped. There was the olm, embedded in the waspgnat's chest. It was the size of a walnut. Now was her chance to save Olive, to save the garden. She knew that she had to get the olm and destroy it, but she didn't want to go anywhere near the waspgnat, let alone touch it.

Suddenly, the waspgnat twisted its hideous face toward her and started to laugh. Bending its rootish limbs backward, it scuttled across the grass toward the hole in the paving stone. Toots dived after it.

"Toots!" screamed her father. "Don't you dare touch that thing!"

But it was too late. With one hand Toots pinned the waspgnat to the ground, while with the other she plucked the olm from its chest.

A horrible scream startled all the birds in the trees and sent them screeching into the sky.

Toots's father grabbed her elbow and yanked her to her feet. He was furious. She hid the heavy purple stone behind her back.

"Toots, don't you ever do that again. That horrible thing might be poisonous." And with that he kicked the waspgnat out of the way. It skidded perilously close to the hole in the paving stone.

The waspgnat wriggled toward the hole. Without the olm it moved more slowly, but it was still very much alive and trying to get back under the ground.

Toots knew what she had to do. The only way to save the garden, to save the fairies, to save Olive, was to destroy the olm before the waspgnat had a chance to grow another.

"Toots, get away," commanded her father. "Go on over by the house. And stay there!"

Toots ran to the side of the house, and Binky followed. She tried her best to crush the olm with her hands, but it was like trying to crush a rock. She hit it against the wall as hard as she could, but that didn't even mark it, let alone make a crack or dent in it. She put it on the ground and smashed a brick on top of it, but still nothing happened. It wasn't even scratched. Toots looked back at the waspgnat. It was closer to the hole now.

She turned the olm over in her hands. The purple stone was as smooth and as hard as a marble. What could she do to get it to break? What could she do?

"Hi, Toots," said a small voice. Toots jumped and looked up. Jemma was standing at the garden gate. Toots didn't say anything. She frowned and would have turned away, but at that moment the olm began to vibrate in her hand.

Toots looked down at it, then up at Jemma. Jemma shrugged and turned away.

Toots watched her set off down the street. As the old annoyed-with-Jemma feeling rose inside her, the olm vibrated even more. Toots knew she was only helping the waspgnat by feeling that way toward her friend. She didn't want to help the waspgnat. She wanted to get rid of it.

Toots closed her hand around the olm and held it tight. *Jemma must have had something very important to do on the day of the car wash*, she told herself. And in a flash she recalled how often she'd seen Jemma going somewhere with her parents on the days that she'd "let her down." *Maybe there's something happening that Jemma doesn't want to or can't tell me about*, she thought. *Maybe that's why she changed the subject when I asked her. Maybe it's something very private.* And in that instant Toots understood what friendship really is. It isn't about doing favors and owing someone something or giving them presents or anything like that. It's about trust and forgiveness and love. Toots opened her eyes.

"Jemma!" she shouted as loud as she could. "Jemma, come back. Please!"

The wind screamed through the garden.

"Jemma!" Toots rushed down the path and flung the gate open wide.

"Jemma!" she called as loudly as she could. "Jemma, please come back!"

The marble-hard olm crumbled in her hand like soft chalk. Toots opened her fingers and a fine purple powder, which was all that was left of the waspgnat's olm, blew away like sand in a storm.

Toots grinned as Jemma hesitantly made her way back to the gate. She wanted to say something welcoming, something that would let Jemma know that she wanted to be friends again, but she didn't get the chance, because at that moment her father yelled excitedly.

"Toots! Toots, quick! Come and look at this."

Toots grabbed Jemma by the hand and pulled her through the gate.

"What is it, Dad?" panted Toots.

Her father raised his eyebrows when he saw Jemma and would probably have said something embarrassing if Toots had given him the chance.

"Dad, what is it?"

"What? Oh, yes, look what's happening to this thing." He pointed at the ground where the waspgnat lay writhing horribly.

Toots watched in fascination as the waspgnat's limbs clawed at the air, then entwined themselves tightly around the pulpy center of its being. It was almost as if it was strangling itself. The root-like limbs looped in and over themselves and squeezed tighter and tighter, and the vile mouth opened and closed wordlessly. The waspgnat had lost its voice.

Soon all that remained of the waspgnat was a small, solid black nugget like a lump of coal, smoldering harmlessly on the ground.

"Well, what do you make of that?" asked Toots's father, prodding the small nugget with the stick.

Mr. Phelps put a glove on his hand, then crouched down and picked up the waspgnat's remains.

"My grandfather once told me of a root like this," he said, examining it. "He said it was a vile thing that could cripple a garden, keep it in winter forever. He said that they grew on bad feelings, that they thrived on anger and hate. Some folks thought my grandfather was mad, that he talked to the fairies. . . . Maybe he did. When I saw this thing come smoking out of the ground, I reckoned that maybe that was what you had. I don't know exactly what she did, but if it hadn't been for your daughter, you would have lost this tree for sure."

Toots felt her cheeks flush. If it hadn't have been for her, the garden would never have been in any danger in the first place.

"What do you mean, *would* have lost the tree?" asked Toots's father. "Is the tree all right now? I don't understand."

Slowly, Toots looked up, and her eyes followed the branches of the horse chestnut tree, where tiny green buds were appearing one by one.

"Dad!" she cried. "Dad, Jemma, look at the tree. Look!"

Her father stared goggle-eyed at the tree.

"Buds," he finally spluttered.

"And there's another and another and another!" Toots shouted, grabbing Jemma's arm and running around the tree.

"And look," laughed her father, pointing to a handful of green shoots that were poking up through the ground.

"And over here, too," added Jemma, pointing at the rose trees.

Binky barked.

"It's a miracle," laughed Toots's father.

"Aye, it is," agreed Mr. Phelps. "A real miracle."

Toots knelt down and felt in her sock for the tiny speck of the wing commander's hankie and wondered if Olive and the fairies would be all right now. . . . She felt sure they would be. Jemma sat down next to her and tugged at the grass.

"You know, I wanted to come and help you that day, but I couldn't," began Jemma. "I had to—"

"That's okay," said Toots. "You don't have to explain. If it was something important, then it was important. It's none of my business. Come on."

Toots jumped to her feet. "Let's play on the swing. Race you to it."

Toots and Jemma played on the swing all that afternoon, taking turns pushing or being pushed, laughing like a couple of monkeys. Toots couldn't remember the last time she'd had so much fun.

And while they played, it seemed that more buds appeared on the tree and more green shot sprang up through the soil. But Toots and Jemma were too busy having fun to notice what was happening in the garden. They were too busy to notice that spring had come at last.

Carol Hughes learned all about great fantasy growing up in England. She now lives in San Francisco with her husband and daughter. *Toots Underground* is Carol's third novel.